DATE DUE			
1/4/11			
MAR 11 2011			
APR 28 2011			

Legend of the Golden Coyote

OTHER FIVE STAR WESTERNS BY MAX BRAND:

The Stone That Shines (1997); *Men Beyond the Law* (1997); *Beyond the Outposts* (1997); *The Fugitive's Mission* (1997); *In the Hills of Monterey* (1998); *The Lost Valley* (1998); *Chinook* (1998); *The Gauntlet* (1998); *The Survival of Juan Oro* (1999); *Stolen Gold* (1999); *The Geraldi Trail* (1999); *Timber Line* (1999); *The Gold Trail* (1999); *Gunman's Goal* (2000); *The Overland Kid* (2000); *The Masterman* (2000); *The Outlaw Redeemer* (2000); *The Peril Trek* (2000); *The Bright Face of Danger* (2000); *Don Diablo* (2001); *The Welding Quirt* (2001); *The Tyrant* (2001); *The House of Gold* (2001); *The Lone Rider* (2002); *Crusader* (2002); *Smoking Guns* (2002); *Jokers Extra Wild* (2002); *Flaming Fortune* (2003); *Blue Kingdom* (2003); *The Runaways* (2003); *Peter Blue* (2003); *The Golden Cat* (2004); *The Range Finder* (2004); *Mountain Storms* (2004); *Hawks and Eagles* (2004); *Trouble's Messenger* (2005); *Bad Man's Gulch* (2005); *Twisted Bars* (2005); *The Crystal Game* (2005); *Dogs of the Captain* (2006); *Red Rock's Secret* (2006); *Wheel of Fortune* (2006); *Treasure Well* (2006); *Acres of Unrest* (2007); *Rifle Pass* (2007); *Melody and Cordoba* (2007); *Outlaws From Afar* (2007); *Rancher's Legacy* (2008); *The Good Badman* (2008); *Love of Danger* (2008); *Nine Lives* (2008); *Silver Trail* (2009); *The Quest* (2009); *Mountain Made* (2009); *Black Thunder* (2009); *Iron Dust* (2010); *The Black Muldoon* (2010); *The Lightning Runner* (2010)

Legend of the Golden Coyote

A WESTERN DUO

MAX BRAND®

FIVE STAR
A part of Gale, Cengage Learning

GALE
CENGAGE Learning™

Detroit • New York • San Francisco • New Haven, Conn • Waterville, Maine • London

GALE
CENGAGE Learning

Five Star Publishing, a part of Gale, Cengage Learning.

Set in 11 pt. Plantin.

LIBRARY OF CONGRESS CATALOGING-IN-PUBLICATION DATA

Brand, Max, 1892–1944.
Legend of the golden coyote : a Western duo / by Max Brand. — 1st ed.
p. cm.
ISBN-13: 978-1-59414-902-3 (hardcover)
ISBN-10: 1-59414-902-X (hardcover)
I. Brand, Max, 1892–1944. Thunder and lightning. II. Title.
PS3511.A87L43 2010
813'.52—dc22 2010034761

First Edition. First Printing: December 2010.
Published in 2010 in conjunction with Golden West Literary Agency.

Printed in the United States of America
1 2 3 4 5 6 7 14 12 11 10

ACKNOWLEDGMENTS

TABLE OF CONTENTS

★ ★ ★ ★ ★

Thunder and Lightning

★ ★ ★ ★ ★

In "Thunder and Lightning" Frederick Faust wrote with a light touch, having fun with his readers, spinning a tale of the timber country in the Paul Bunyan tradition, employing a down-to-earth, folksy narrative style that perfectly fits his overtly melodramatic subject matter. Celebrating the strength of two massive lumbermen, Almayer and Clarges, these titans inevitably move toward one another to clash in the kind of mythic battle Faust excelled at describing. Never previously reprinted and now with its original title restored, the story first appeared as "Lightning Lumberjacks" under the John Frederick byline in the March 12, 1927 issue of *Western Story Magazine.*

I

Up in our part of the world we used to say that the reason that Jimmy Clarges and Soapy Almayer teamed it together and were such good partners was because they were afraid not to be friends. I mean that each of them could lick all the rest of the world, you understand. And each of them *had* licked all the rest of the world, as you might say. All that was left was each other. I wasn't on hand when Clarges came hunting for Almayer to get his scalp, and when Almayer came clean across the mountains to eat up Clarges. But they met one day in a little one-horse town, and the minute that they laid eyes on one another, they began to slow up. And you wouldn't wonder.

Each of them was made just opposite. Soapy Almayer was four and a half inches above six feet in his bare feet, and he weighed two and a half hundred pounds. He was blond and handsome in a sort of a terrible, bold way, if you know what I mean. And Jimmy Clarges was three inches under six feet, but still he weighed a shade more than Soapy. He was not fat—just knotted and deformed with muscle. His hands came nearly to his knees. No neck could hold his head. It just was laid on his shoulders like a bowl on a shelf. He had a long, lean, ugly, pale face down to the jaw that was made like the prow of a battleship. Soapy was kind of glorious, and Jimmy was kind of nightmarish.

There was a sad look in the eyes of each of them, folks said, until they met one another. There was a sad look, the saying went, because neither of them could find a man to fight. But, when they saw each other, the sad light went out of their eyes. It wasn't a question of one of them backing down. It was just a question of each of them seeing that the other was dynamite. And not even a fool will step on powder.

So they began to team together, and what they did in company was to be told, but hardly to be believed. Most storytellers like to have a theme so that they can expand on it, but there was no question of expanding on Almayer and Clarges. You had to trim your story fine and undershoot the mark, or else the folks that didn't know about the pair would laugh in your face.

I'd heard about them, of course, but I'd never seen them, till one day they walked into the lumber camp, along about evening time. They came out of the woods like a pair of bull moose. They walked up to the superintendent and asked for a job.

"Do you know timber?" he said.

"No," said Almayer.

"Can you pick up ideas?" said the big boss.

"No," said Almayer.

"Then what can you do for me?" the boss demanded.

"Work," said Almayer, and he held out his hands.

Gloves were never made that would fit Almayer. The boss looked down at those hands, and then he looked at the shoulders of Clarges.

"I guess I can use you," he said.

"We guessed that maybe you could," said Soapy.

Not boastful, you understand. Just stating the facts. When they got started to work the next morning, we saw what they meant. They couldn't be given the jobs that required skill, but there is plenty of horse work around a lumber camp. I'll never forget when the pair of them was given a big saw and told to get to work with it. In a few minutes they quit, and Almayer came

to me, for I was straw boss over them and some others besides.

"Me and Jimmy are getting cold working that little saw," he said. "He'll take that saw for himself. Gimme another one, kid."

I gave him another one, and he set to work. It was tough, pitchy pine that a saw of any kind hates to work through. There was plenty of flaws and streaks and knots in that wood. And two men had plenty of work dragging a saw through. But not these fellows. I watched Clarges pumping a white stream of sawdust out at either end as he whipped the big saw through the trunk. And it cost him so little effort that, as he worked it, he began to sing. It was not a smooth voice, but out there in the woods it sounded like an organ blowing. It drowned the whining and groaning of the saws. Pretty soon, over the bass of Clarges, Almayer struck into the chorus with a really fine tenor-baritone that made the echoes ring, you bet. They sang, and they worked. And every hour each of them did what would have been a full day's labor for any other strong man. I never saw such a pair.

When noon came, they came in for chow, and then all of us could sit around and wonder for a different reason. Almayer took two quarts of baked beans and a loaf of brown bread for a starter. Jimmy Clarges sat down to a gallon of mulligan. And they polished off their portions, and then came back for more. Each of them ate like three men, and the big boss said to me: "We can't feed those fellows. They'll eat us out!"

"Let 'em eat," I replied. "They'll turn all that fodder into energy before the afternoon is over."

They did, too, until Soapy's saw got stuck. He gave it a jerk and a lunge, and that tough steel blade snapped square off. He came to me carrying the fragments.

"Have you got a real, man-size saw?" he asked.

Well, that was the way that they started in the camp. We learned the very first day to respect and to value them. And before the week was over, we accepted them as fine fellows.

Friday night a big Canuck came into camp full of moonshine, and started to make trouble. He tripped around the circle over the feet of the jacks, cussed them off, told what a great man-eater he was, and begged somebody to come out and fight him. There were men in that camp that would have fought the Canadian, but they didn't step out. They waited, because they felt that this was no time for them to do the hero act. And pretty soon the Canuck came to where Soapy Almayer was lying rolled in a blanket, asleep. He hauled off and kicked Soapy.

"Get up, you fat pig! Fight!" he commanded.

Soapy got up, took the Canuck by the collar and the seat of the pants, and chucked him through the air like a sack of bran to where Jimmy Clarges was sitting.

Jimmy stretched out his arms and gathered the Canadian in.

"Throw this rubbish away for me, Jimmy, will you?" said Soapy. And he lay back down and went on with his nap.

Jimmy Clarges stood up. It wasn't the difference in weight. That big Canuck must have been within fifteen pounds of Jimmy, but he had turned to pulp under the grip of Soapy. Now Clarges just grabbed him by the neck and dragged him out of camp. And the Canuck hung limply, screaming for help. Clarges took him to the bank of the river. We heard a splash, and we knew that the Canuck had had a chance to cool off his moonshine in water fresh from the snows. But neither Clarges nor Soapy prided themselves on that. They never referred to the Canuck again, and, when anybody else mentioned him, they yawned.

We liked the pair of them fine. They were big without being overbearing. They were strong without taking advantage of anybody. I mean that they didn't take advantage of anybody in important things. But, just the same, they had a rather irritating way until you got used to it. They took certain things for granted. They felt that the best place on the windward of the fire ought to be theirs, and that they should be allowed to sleep an extra hour in the morning, and that they should have the grub that they wanted.

The pair of them had what they wanted, without any questions asked, until another gent came into camp and started trouble. Certainly you never would have thought, to see him, that he was the man to make trouble for a pair of giants like Almayer and Clarges. He was almost five feet eight, I suppose, but, up there in that lumber camp, where the smallest man shaded six feet as a rule, he looked hardly more than a boy. Some of the fellows started calling him Skinny, but that was changed to Shorty, and he was let down at that. He was right off the range, wearing high-heeled boots and a neckerchief and all the rest. Although he took off his gun belt after the first day, and put off his holster, too, still you could always see the bulge of his Colt on him, where it was stowed away under his clothes. You take a cattleman, and he ain't happy without a gun. Deprive him of his gun, and it's like robbing an ordinary man of his eyesight or his hearing.

Shorty got a job and stuck to it. He was very quiet and made no trouble at all until the third day, I think it was, after he arrived, when lunch time came. That was the main meal. Along about 12:00 P.M., you would see the lumberjacks coming in from the woods, with the steam from their nostrils floating behind them in the crisp mountain air. And right in the first of the rush was sure to be a pair of giants, shoulder to shoulder. That day, the pair of them was a little late for some reason. When they came in, they found that the bench opposite the center of the table was sort of full. Soapy found room to squeeze himself in. Jimmy Clarges took the next man under the armpits and lifted him right off the bench and sat down in his place, saying: "Give a man room, kid, will you?"

The rest of us sort of grinned, seeing Shorty snatched out of his place, that way, but the next moment we stopped our grinning, I can tell you, because Shorty's voice barked sharp and high, like the voice of a terrier.

"Stand up, you fat-headed sap!"

II

You don't know how it sounded. It made me want to laugh, until I craned my neck and saw the twisted, white face of Shorty. He was frantic. But what could he mean by fighting? We saw in another minute, for Soapy picked up a half loaf of bread and chucked it over his shoulder, saying: "Eat that, kid, and don't talk foolish."

That bread was stopped in mid-flight through the air and came right back at Soapy. A gun had jumped into the hand of Shorty and spoke. As that half loaf glanced off the head of Soapy and tumbled onto the table, we couldn't help observing the hole that was blown through it. A .45 chips out a pretty big chunk, where it lights. And, just then, that hole through the loaf seemed to me like a bullet through a man's vitals.

I looked at it and looked at Shorty, then I looked back at Soapy. No, it wasn't any joke. There had been gunfighters around that neck of the woods before, but there had never been a fellow who could snap a gun out of his clothes and pop small things as they drifted across through the air.

Soapy turned around with a roar, leaped out of his place, and started for Shorty. But Shorty didn't run. He stood in his tracks with fire in his eyes, and the gun hanging at his side.

"Get out your gat, you thickheaded bull!" he yelled at Soapy. "Get out your gat because, if you try to handle me with bare fingers, I'll tear you to pieces."

Soapy didn't pause. He couldn't. And you couldn't imagine a giant like that really pulling up at all on account of such a little thing as a revolver.

I expected the next minute to see that gun's muzzle twitch up, and a jet of smoke and fire dart from it. But the gun didn't stir. There wasn't time, for, just then, a shadow sailed in between Soapy and the kid.

It was the big bench that the men had jumped up from and that Jimmy Clarges had heaved up to help his pal. That bench hit Shorty and bowled him over, while the second bullet from his gun punched a nice, clear hole in the blue of the sky.

Then he lay still, and Soapy ran on and picked the kid up in his arms.

"What d'ye mean?" he yelled to Clarges. "What d'ye mean spoiling my little party?"

"You fool," said Clarges, "ain't you ever going to learn that a Colt ain't a popgun?"

"What could it have done to me . . . a little thing like one bullet?" asked Soapy Almayer. "And here you've killed the kid, sure."

By the ugly look of the blood that was streaming down Shorty's face, you would have said that was the case, and that the kid was done for. But, when we swabbed off the blood, we saw that it was only a shallow scalp wound just above the forehead. Then he came to, and he came to raging. He reached out for his gun, no doubt. And then he saw that he had missed his Colt, and, at the same time, he laid eyes on Almayer. You would have thought that he had gone mad, to hear the yell that he let out. He wriggled right through my fingers, very snaky and fast, and rushed for the giant. Yes, sir, tackled him bare-handed!

It was an amazing thing to see. Soapy reached out a hand to brush Shorty away, as you would have brushed away a fly. The cowpuncher dipped under that swinging arm and rammed four full-speed punches into the pit of the big boy's stomach as fast as he could slam them. Then, as Soapy tried to gather the kid in, Shorty ducked out again, and the spat of his knuckles on the face of Soapy was like the clapping together of bare hands. They were not easy punches, either. When a man knows how to hit, he can hurt anyone in the world, no matter how big. There was a snarl beginning to form in the hollow of Soapy's throat. In another moment, I suppose he would have clinched with the kid and smashed him, but here the big boss stepped in and laid a hand on the kid's shoulder.

Shorty tossed him a glance, and then lowered his hands.

"He insulted me," said Shorty, his face twitching. "And now I get a chance to fight him, or I'll know the reason why."

"Leave him go," said Soapy, nodding. "He's a game little chicken, and I won't hurt him. Let him have his place on the bench, if he wants. He deserves it." And he felt one of the bumps that was rising on his face and laughed a little. It just tickled him that any man had dared to stand up to him.

"I can have my place, can I?" snapped the kid. Then he whirled around and pointed a finger at Jimmy Clarges. "You're on my books, too, you lump of nothing," he stated.

Oh, he was in a fighting humor, that Shorty was. It did me good to listen to him rip into the pair of them. But then the big boss led him away. I went along.

The boss said: "Kid, you're game, and you had something to fight about. But you're wrong, just the same."

"Show me where," said Shorty.

"Clarges and Almayer mean no harm. It's only that they have an overbearing way with them. Besides, I don't allow guns in this camp."

"Then I'm through with your camp and you, too," spat Shorty. "And tell the pair of them, after you've paid me off, that I'm going to trim them down to the quick. I'm going to make them wish that they'd never seen my face."

The boss tried to smooth him down, and said that he didn't

want to lose him, and that we all respected him for the way that he'd acted, and that Almayer and Clarges respected him, too. But that wouldn't work. Nothing would please that kid except a chance to fight it out with the pair of them.

"Give 'em to me one at a time," he said, "with knives, clubs, or anything they please. Or with a gun, I'll take on the pair of them."

Nothing else would suit him. He even offered to fight them bare-handed. But, of course, the boss was too sensible to allow that. So he had to pay off the kid, who went away through the woods, the hottest youngster that you ever seen in your life.

The boss said to me: "This ain't the end of this fracas. We'll hear some more about Shorty before we're done with him, and I'd like to bet that we curse the day that we ever saw him."

I felt much the same about it, because there was distilled essence of poison in that Shorty. He meant mean work, and I didn't doubt that he would find some way of harming all of us. I never guessed, though, the way that he would choose. None of us could do that, it was so roundabout and clever.

After Shorty left, things settled down in the camp and went along extra fine and smooth. Almayer and Clarges had had a lesson that did them good, and, from that time on, they didn't rough the boys or shoulder them out of the way at all. They seemed to understand that mere bulk was not all that there was to a man. In the meantime, they worked harder than ever. They had picked up a lot of the tricks of the lumber trade by this time. How much they added to the good cheer of that camp it would be hard to say. For one thing, there was no lack of men in the camp that season. Usually the boys fell away when the cold weather hit us, but this season there was a steady drift of gents up to the camp, eager and anxious to have a chance to see the two giants. And, after they came, they stayed, because it was a sight to see Almayer and Clarges, or to hear them sing, or to watch them eating more like a pair of horses than a pair of men.

In fact, we had to be turning hands away all of the time, and the work was pushed ahead with a vim that surprised me. I had been five years on that job, and I'd never heard of such progress as was being made now. The big boss laid it all to Almayer and Clarges. Of course, we got a nickname for them. Saying their names, one by one, was too hard work for a Western memory. And one day, when they were singing in the distance, with the chime of their axes clinking in between the rhythm, a lumberjack sang out: "Listen to thunder and lightning!" It did make you think of that—the bumbling and rumbling of Clarges's bass, and the higher, cleaner-cut ring of the voice of Almayer.

After that, we called them Thunder and Lightning, and a good name it was for them. It hitched them up proper, and, from that time, they were never known in any other way through the lumber camps and over the whole spread of the cow camps in the lower hills. So we went along with everything as merry as you please until, all at once, the trouble hit us. No, not all at once, but gradually.

Who ever heard of an invitation to a dance being the start of fighting? That was the way of it, however. Because one day at lunch time an old chap rode a pony into camp and sang out that down in the town there was a dance the next Saturday night and would us boys come down? They were bringing up a lot of extra girls from all over the range, and it was thought that there would be two hundred couples dancing in the assembly room of the old town hall. It sounded good to us. It sounded terrible good. And, from that time on, there wasn't much except waiting for the day of the dance, you can bet.

And Almayer and big Clarges? You would think that they would never dream of stepping out like a couple of elephants on a dance floor and two-stepping or waltzing with a girl. But that's where you would be wrong, as we were all wrong. No really little man seems to know just how foolish and small he is, and no really big man seems to know just how foolish and big he is.

III

Saturday evening there was a rush through dinner. Nobody seemed to care much what sort of nourishment he got. And, when we were all turned out for the dance, we got a sensation that staggered us a mite. When we were all tumbling into the buckboards that the big boss had supplied to cart us down to the dance, out came big Soapy Almayer and Jimmy Clarges, side-by-side, and they were dressed up like a pair of bandwagons. Jimmy had on golden-red corduroys, while his trousers were shoved into red boots. It looked like there must have been a whole calfskin used for the making of each of those boots. He had a great blue silk sash around his waist, a shirt of yellow silk, too, and a red-and-blue necktie. When Jimmy stepped out in that outfit, you could see him clear enough. You didn't have to have him pointed out to you, as that being the man. You could have seen him through a fog. You could have heard him like a church bell, he was that loud.

But everything goes by comparison and, compared with Soapy, I got to admit that Clarges was sort of pale and insignificant. I would hate to say that he didn't amount to nothing, but the fact is that it was pretty hard to see Jimmy at all, when he was walking along there with his friend. For one thing, there was a lot more of Soapy. I mean, looking up and down, there was. There was just as many square yards of surface on Jimmy to take your attention. Soapy was loftier. He could carry his flag higher, as you might say.

Well, on the top of that head of his, set onto the pale golden hair that he had and wore long, Soapy had a purple cap, round and sort of woolly, and there was a long yellow tassel to set it off and flop around, when he talked or shook his head, or anything like that. That was just the beginning of what Soapy had on. He wasn't wearing long boots, like Jimmy. But somebody had come up through the mountains selling shoes made of a kind of soft yellow leather. They were comfortable and fitted fine, but they didn't last long. Soapy had polished up those boots of his and worked over them, until they shone like they had been varnished. And almost the first thing that you would see about him would be the two spots of yellow—one on top of his head, and the other on his feet. Not that there wasn't other things to see in between his head and his feet. Soapy had a dead-black suit. It was the blackest and the deadest-looking thing that you ever saw, and, under the coat, by way of a belt, he wore a broad, orange scarf. Since he always kept his coat open, the thing that you saw all the time was sure to be the orange scarf. I never saw such a color. There was a blue shirt on Soapy that was pretty intense. You could see it by its own light, so to speak. And there was a scarlet tie around his neck that talked for itself, too. But nothing seemed to matter, somehow, except that flaring, flaming, burning sash of orange that he wore around his middle. It was just as though you had picked up a great big banner of living fire and knotted it around the middle of big Soapy Almayer.

They were pretty conscious that they were magnificent. The pair of them looked down very kindly and patronizing on all of the rest of us. It seemed like Soapy had some more finery left in his bedding roll. He was a good-natured gent, with a heart as big as a mountain, and he just couldn't stand seeing the boys of his own camp fixed out so cheap and poor as we were. He wanted us to go right over to his roll and there to help ourselves to anything that we could find. Clarges offered the same.

I managed to duck them by saying that it was late already,

and that we'd better start. So off we rolled down the mountain, along what was called a road by the grace of God and a sense of humor.

Jimmy and Soapy were, of course, sitting side-by-side. I was behind them and could watch what was going on. They loved each other better than brothers, you had better believe. But, just now, they were envying each other so bad that they could hardly stand it. What would make them jealous? Why, there was one thing on each of them that seemed to bust up his pal. The fine, shining boots of Jimmy Clarges was what made Soapy groan. And Jimmy, when he looked at that orange-colored belt of Soapy's, could hardly stand it. He just shook his head and looked sick.

"I cottoned to that sash the first time that I saw it," Clarges said finally. "I might have known that I needed it. But who will look at a sawed-off runt like me, unless I got something to set me off and catch the eye? But I left you to buy that scarf, Soapy, because it got your eye."

"H-m-m," said Soapy.

There was a long silence, so gloomy that pretty soon I thought that there would be a smash between the two of them, and it made me hang onto the edges of my seat, fearing that that pair of giants might grab one another and manage to wreck us all in their struggles.

But soon Soapy said: "I would sort of be ashamed, Jimmy, to envy another gent some little thing that he might happen to have. I would sort of be ashamed, if I had what you got."

"What have I got?" asked Jimmy.

"Now," said Soapy, "you are leading me on, and all the time you're pretending that you don't know. But you *do* know. And this here dodge won't work."

"Soapy, old man," said Clarges, "I give you my word that I dunno what you're speaking about. I never was fixed up so miserable for a long time, when going to a party."

"Bah!" Soapy said. "I suppose that those boots of yours ain't anything at all?"

"These?" asked Clarges. He stuck out his leg, big and thick as the trunk of a tree and hard as iron with muscle. "These little old boots?" continued Clarges, wondering. "I dunno that anyone would notice them."

"They've got the world beat, those boots," said Soapy, and he sighed again.

Pretty soon there was a sudden start from Jimmy. Then he leaned over and worked for a minute. After a while he sat up with a grunt. He had peeled off his boots, and now he handed them across to Soapy.

"Here, kid," he said. "I couldn't get no happiness out of them boots now that you've taken to hankering after them."

It amazed me a good deal to hear that. And Soapy, he was like a sick man.

"What you doing, Jim?" he asked. "Put them boots back on, will you? Put them back on. Why, darned if you ain't shaming me, Jimmy. How could I be taking the shoes off of your own feet?"

"I'll wear yours, and glad to have 'em. I always had a hankering after yellow, old boy."

"Do you mean that?"

"I give you my word."

"Solemn and faithful, kid?"

"Sure."

"I think you're a liar, Jimmy."

"Soapy, old heart, I mean it. I would be the happiest man in the camp, if you was to let me have them yellow shoes of yours."

"I'm a mean, low skunk to do this," said Soapy. "But if you really think that maybe you would just as soon wear these yellow shoes tonight . . . why, here they are."

He yanked off his shoes on the double-quick, and Jimmy put them on. Soapy jerked on the red boots, and he sat and admired them for a long while. The gent that was sitting next to me in the buckboard, behind the pair of giants, he beat me black and blue, to keep me from busting out laughing.

"Wait a minute," Soapy said a bit later as we was sliding in a broadside skid around the edge of the road and hanging on the rim of a precipice. "Wait a minute. Dog-gone me if I didn't forget something."

"What is it, Soapy?"

"I forgot that you were admiring this here sash that I'm wearing. Here, Jimmy, you take this, will you?"

"Hey, Soapy, what're you doing? Don't you be a fool. That there scarf is about the finest-looking thing that I ever seen you have on."

"Is it?" Soapy said with a sort of a groan. "Well, I don't believe you. I never liked this here thing . . . never give a hang for this sash. But it might look fine on you with your get-up, Jimmy. Here. You try it."

"Soapy, if I was to get my hands on that scarf, I dunno that it would be at all easy for me to give it up ag'in."

"Who would be asking it from you? No, you take that scarf and keep it."

"I'm a mean hound if I do, Soapy."

"You ain't nothing of the kind."

So soon Jimmy Clarges took the orange-colored scarf and gave Soapy his own big, blue sash. They knotted those scarves around themselves, and they drove on very happy and hunky-dory, and before long they felt so good—one about the scarf, and one about the shoes—that they couldn't help busting into a song, each with his monster big arm thrown around the shoulders of the other.

Down that mountainside we went with the thunder of that

music around us, till we seen the lights of the town twinkle and then rise up before us. Then we were rolling through the streets of the little village, and gents were shouting to us from the sidewalks, and riders were swishing by, and rigs were rolling up and down, and you could just feel by the nip in the air that one of the best times that you ever heard about was coming up

IV

The town hall was a corker. It had been built when folks had an idea that Elk's Crossing was going to grow up into a real city, and so the miners were real forehanded, as you might say, and they arranged to have a hall that would be able to house the most bang-up city government that ever was heard about. They started right at the bottom and went up. At the bottom they had laid out a fine big lawn that covered the whole square, and in the lawn they had planted palms and such like things. Then, in the middle of the lawn, they had laid out sites for two big fountain bowls, and in between the fountain bowls stood the building. It was square, and it had in front of it columns of real white marble that was taken out from the marble quarry up back in the hills.

Well, the lawn was only working in patches, now. And the fountains were busted, and their bowls were filled with drift and blow-sand. The palm trees, they looked pretty meager, their heads were like a cabbage that a chicken has scratched to pieces. Just the same, with the night to cover things up, and with the lights flaring in the entrance, and the tall, white columns standing up big and grand before the house, it was a fine thing to see. But then you got closer, and you seen the places where the plaster had peeled off, and you seen the cracks in the wall, and the ornery-looking people that were going in and out and standing smoking and laughing around the door, and you knew that, after all, this was where you belonged.

It made quite some considerable sensation when Thunder and Lightning arrived. Everybody turned and stared at them, and, when the lights flashed over 'em, you had better believe that they were worth staring at. They walked into that courthouse like two pillars of fire, and the small boys of the town were out, watching the folks come and go at the dance. Those boys made a rush and piled in after the pair of them and followed Thunder and Lightning up the stairs. It was a great show. Nobody was mean tempered about the kids breaking in. They just laughed and let it go, and kicked the kids out as hard as they could kick.

There were Thunder and Lightning standing at last in the middle of the assembly room in the courthouse of Elk's Crossing. It was a whopping big room with a huge, high ceiling. The walls were so high that the ceiling looked hardly more than half as big as the floor. It was funny to stand and look at them. Around the walls there were the chairs with the girls sitting in them. Some folks like the girls along the seashore—the sailor girls, and such—and some take to the girls on the plains and the farms, and some have a fancy for the girls off of the cow range. But me, speaking personally, I say, gimme every time the girls from the mountains . . . where a girl grows up tall and straight and not too talky . . . where, when she smiles, it means something . . . and when she laughs it pretty near stops your heart . . . and where every girl you meet don't look as if you could tell her that you loved her and get away with it. You know what I mean. Not that they were offish, but that they had some dignity. They weren't mulish. No, they were downright pleasant, but they had sense. In a word, they weren't just wall decorations—they were women.

I looked them over. There was a stirring and whirling around of men in front of them, men asking for dances and getting acquainted. There were the floor managers hiking around and making introductions as fast as they could talk. When I looked over that open square of girls' faces, I leaned against the wall with one hand and I fanned myself with the other. I felt like a kid that is brought before a Christmas tree all loaded down with wonderful things and told to take his pick. Because they all looked so fine—those girls, I mean.

Just at that minute, as though they had been waiting for the arrival of Thunder and Lightning before starting, the orchestra hit up the first dance. That was some orchestra. I wish that you could have heard it. The fat man in the corner was the drummer. And he had more noise-making contraptions than you ever heard in your life. Wonderful how he could work them, too. He could hit a bass drum with his heel, a gong with his toe, and a cymbal with his elbow all at the same time, while he was ringing a bell with one hand and beating a snare drum with the other and blowing a train whistle that was fixed between his teeth. You see, there are some that can get to be musicians by a lot of hard work. And I admire them for their hard work, and all. But you take a fellow like that drummer, it was just plain genius. I got to take my hat off to a man like that. He was pretty fat, and so, when he got sort of tired, he had a boy along with him to strike in and work the traps. The kid was clever, too, and had a fine teacher in the fat man. But work as he would, that kid didn't have the genius. He couldn't get the bursts of noise in on the right spots to help you around the corner with your girl, or to make you spin at the right time.

I wouldn't let you think, though, that orchestra was made up of a drummer and nothing else. No, sir, that was really a mighty refined orchestra, as anybody could tell, because nothing but really swell orchestras have a violin and a flute in 'em. But this one did. Besides that, it had five other instruments, which was two real, hang-up sliding trombones and a saxophone that would send a shudder right down your spine, and a wonderful tenor cornet that you hear right over everything except the trombones. In addition, there was a great big bass horn that made the floor tremble and turn to water under your feet. That was the orchestra that struck up just as we entered and got a good look around us.

When the music started, you could hear a roar of feet on the stairs, as the boys all started on the rush to claim the girls that they had booked dances with. I didn't wait for that tidal wave to hit me. I ducked in fast. There wasn't much time for picking and choosing, but what was the need when they was all so fine? I seen a girl with a blue dress on and freckles across her nose, and I sashayed up to her and said: "Your brother says that I'm to dance this one with you, Miss Gulliver."

"My name ain't Gulliver," she said. "And besides. . . ."

"All right," I responded. "No matter about a little thing like a name. I got to be seen by your brother doing my duty and dancing with a girl."

"But I ain't got a brother."

"That's all right," I said, "Miss Gulliver has one."

"I don't understand you."

"You will before the dance is over," I said, pulling her up out of her chair by both hands.

She was the owner of a plumb-crooked smile that knocked a dimple right into the middle of one cheek. Amazing! She turned that grin loose on me, and my knees sagged.

"Besides . . . ," she began.

But just then that blessed drummer, he hit an inspired place in his system, and uncorked a lot of whistles and bangs and whangs and bumps that just tickled a man's feet right into moving. That girl, she couldn't help letting me take her in my arms and whirl her away.

"You was about to say something," I asked.

"I dunno what."

"It begun with 'besides,' " I told her.

"Oh, yes," she said. "I was about to say that I couldn't dance this one with you because I had it already with another man."

"Hey," I said, weakening a little, "why didn't you say that before?"

It ain't an easy thing, when you cut out a cowpuncher from his dance. Most usually he wants to break you in two because of it. But then I took another look at her.

"All right," I said. "I'll fix it with him."

"He's a very mean man."

"Oh, that's all right."

She looked up at me and puckered her brows. And then the dimple sunk into one cheek. It wouldn't've pleased her to see a couple of gents fighting about her. Oh, no. Not at all, it wouldn't.

"But," she said, "you belong to Thunder and Lightning, don't you?"

"Lady, what might your name be?"

"Jessica Long," she answered.

"Jessica, don't you make no mistake. Thunder and Lightning belong to *me!*"

"Oh," she asked, "are you one of the bosses?"

"I am."

Well, she settled down into my arms and gave me a happy look as much as to say: "Let the world rip. I got what I want out of it."

Women is that way; maybe you happen to know. I mean, they're sold out to gents that have got a position, or something. They like a gent that has got power. Even a straw boss in a lumber camp is something. That was me!

V

You would think that I had forgotten about Thunder and Lightning. But I haven't forgotten about them at all. I just wanted only to take things pretty slow and easy for a while. I wanted to show you about that girl, Jessica. I mean to say, she was a humdinger. She *is* a humdinger. I never have met anybody like her. She deserved a little space all to herself. But now I'll get back to Thunder and Lightning and to something else.

While I was circling around the room with Jessica, hitting it up high and lively, over in a corner I saw a gent about average size, with wide shoulders and a mighty graceful way of dancing. He was got up modestly in dark clothes, with no smart dashes of color about him, but his easy way of dancing and something else about him made him quick to notice. I seen his back first and the face of the girl that was dancing with him. She was something extra. She was a cut above me.

What I mean to say is, Jessica was pretty, dressed up fine, and a bang-up dancer. But this other girl, she was a queen. She had a pair of eyes that picked you up and set you down again. She had a sort of a pale face, kind of Mexican olive, when you looked at it close, and very black hair—tons of it. But nothing that I could say about her would tell you what she was.

Maybe you have seen a good deal of horses. Standing together, they look pretty much the same, and you look over the lot and place your bets, but when they come out and the race starts, you suddenly see one of them that has the action and the way of going and the looks all tied together, and you know that that's the winner. That was the way with this girl. She was the winner, no matter what sort of company she was placed in. And just as I got over the shock of seeing her, her partner whirled her around, and I seen his face, and that was another shock because it was Shorty.

Shorty there in the same dance hall with Thunder and Lightning! And Shorty, of course, had a gun or two stowed on his person. You just couldn't imagine that little fire-eater without a Colt or two packed away on him.

Jessica seen that I was rather worked up, and in one glance she seen why.

"She's awfully pretty," Jessica said. "There isn't anybody else like her, is there?"

She said it without being spiteful, or without sort of asking you to praise her and run down the other girl. You see, that was the kind that the other one was.

"What's her name?" I asked.

"Rosita Alvarado."

"And what is the name of the gent that's dancing with her?" I asked.

"That's Jack Thomas."

"Do you know anything about him?"

"No. He just hit town a few days ago."

"And what's he doing?"

"Working on the Alvarado place, riding range."

"You mean that's the daughter of his boss?"

"Yes."

"He seems to get along with her pretty well."

"He's a grand dancer, ain't he?" Jessica asked, looking him over. "I guess he's quite a man, maybe."

Women have got an instinct to pick a horse. They've got an instinct to pick a man, too. And I knew that she was right, and that Shorty was quite a man. But, just the same, I was pretty sure that there was going to be trouble between this Shorty and Thunder and Lightning. I could feel it in my bones. In the meantime, there was something else to think about. That was Thunder and Lightning themselves. They had got themselves partners, and they had stepped out to dance.

It was a funny thing to watch Jimmy Clarges; he had picked out the tallest girl in the room, bar none. She stood just as high as he did, and her hair was worn piled up and made her look a good deal taller. And along with big Soapy Almayer there was one of the smallest girls in the room. I don't think that she was an inch more than five feet, but she was mighty pretty and neat. Soapy, you could see, was crazy about her. She was so small, and he was so big that he had to bend over a lot to take hold of her. She had to tilt back and look almost straight up to the ceiling to talk to him. It made you laugh to look at them. But as she was dancing with a gent that everybody knew the name of, you could see that she didn't much care what sort of a picture she made with him. She was happy, and Soapy Almayer . . . he was just blind happy with her.

"Ain't he a fine, big, simple fellow?" Jessica said to me, laughing.

"He sure is," I replied.

You could tell that everybody in the room had taken a liking to Thunder and Lightning.

But after that dance was over, I put Jessica into a corner. And I said to her: "Jessica, how are you staked out for this evening? Will you tell me?"

"I have got a pretty crowded program," she admitted, and she looked up to me with a pucker in her forehead.

I said: "Lemme see your program."

She gave it to me, and there it was, all lines and filled with names. There wasn't a single vacant space. And almost every other place was taken by "Charley."

"Who's Charley?" I asked.

"Charley is an old friend," Jessica said, a little red.

It sort of stopped my heart. Charley—well, blast Charley. Then I tore that program up and dropped it into my pocket.

"Good gracious!" she exclaimed, her eyes popping. "What have you done?"

"I'll tell you," I explained. "While you was leaning at the window, over there, dog-gone me if a puff of wind didn't come along and snatch that program right out of your hand, and so you're all mixed up about your partners."

"I don't know what you mean!"

"Maybe you'll understand later on," I said. "Meantime, you just save every other dance for me. The ones in between you can scatter out among the rest of the boys to please yourself."

"Thank you," she said.

"Oh, that's all right."

"And what might your name be?" she asked.

"Jim Rankin."

"Jim," she told me, "of all the gents in the range, you're the sassiest that I ever did meet."

"The dance after next is the first one that I come back for," I stated, and I went off and left her.

Before I'd taken three steps a big chap comes up to me and glowers down on me, and he said: "Who might you be?"

Well, I didn't have to ask him who *he* was. It was Charley. And he was turned clean batty, he was so mad. I looked him over, and then I remembered Jessica's dimple, and I decided that she was worth trouble.

"Partner," I said, "I take it that you're her man?"

"I dunno about that," he said. "But what I'd like to know is. . . ."

"Hold on," I said. "We can arrange this here thing two ways. We can cut aces to see who leaves this hall tonight, or else we can step outside and shoot it out. Now, you take your choice."

He looked me in the eye. "You're a crusty little hound," he said.

"I ain't so small. I look to myself big enough to handle you."

He just laughed down at me. "All right, kid," he said. "I don't pull shooting irons for Jessica nor no other woman unless I have to. But if we can get a pack of cards, I'll cut with you."

No, he wasn't taking water. By the cut of him, I knew that he was a hundred percent fighting man, and a good man, too. But

wrong, and I take it back. I'm having one fine, large time right now, and I wouldn't let nothing interfere with it."

"All right," I said, taking him at his word. "Over there is Shorty, that you had the trouble with in camp."

He walled his eyes in that direction, and, when he seen Shorty, his nostrils flared out, but then he grinned. "What have I got ag'in' Shorty?" he asked. "Shorty is all right. Shorty is absolutely OK, as far as I'm concerned. We played a mean trick on him, by his way of thinking, and he stood up and sassed us for it. Well, that's all right."

"He punched you in the face, Soapy," I said, looking at the purple spots where those hard punches had landed.

"Love pats," Soapy said. "What did they amount to for me? Nothing at all! That's a game kid, and I sort of like him. Funny thing, though, about Jimmy Clarges."

"Hold on . . . what's he got so bad against Shorty?" I asked. Because I hadn't thought that Jimmy would make any trouble about Shorty at all—him having had the easy end of the fight.

"Well, sir," Soapy said, "Jimmy says that Shorty would have murdered me with his Colt, if he'd had a chance, and Jimmy takes that kind of hard. I dunno that he could keep himself from reaching out and tying the runt into a couple of knots if he was to see him up here tonight."

"You get to Jimmy right away," I suggested to Soapy, "and you explain what a terrible disgrace it would be for a gent to do anything like fighting up here, will you?"

He nodded and grinned and started away to find Clarges. I hadn't explained the most important thing of all to Soapy. Which was that if either him or Jimmy tried to put a hand on Shorty, they would probably get a couple of .45-caliber slugs of lead crashing through their midsection. I hadn't said anything like that, because if I had, the game might have looked sort of attractive to the pair of them. As it was, Shorty was just a foolish kid, game, but wrong, and they could afford to sort of overlook him. You understand my drift, maybe?

I watched Soapy go up to Clarges and hold him back from a dance and talk to him. It made a wonderful picture, the pair of them togged out so gaudy, and with big Soapy draping his hand over the huge, wide shoulder of Jimmy, and Jimmy Clarges looking up to the face of Soapy like an ordinary man, listening to a hero's voice. Other people noticed that picture, and there was a chuckle and a shaking of heads all around the room. There was five hundred weight of muscle and bone standing together in that spot, with enough power to break open heads of men like walnuts, and it was sort of touching to see how plumb fond of each other they was, and how brotherly, and all that, you understand?

It was plain that Soapy was having a hard job of it, because Jimmy kept shaking his head and frowning terrible black, but finally he began to nod, and the pair of them set sail across the room, Soapy leading. I seen that they was heading straight for Shorty, and I tagged along with my heart in my mouth.

I was up close enough to hear what was said. Shorty got up and left the beautiful Rosita, and he stepped out and met them. Soapy said: "Kid, are you here with hard feelings ag'in' us, or ain't you?"

Shorty looked them over and up and down, as cool as you please, and he said to them: "Soapy, I'll never rest till I'm squared up with you. And the same goes for you, Clarges. Someday, I'll be even with you."

With that, he turned his back on 'em and walked back to Rosita Alvarado.

Soapy and his pal were dumbfounded. I suppose that little speech that they had made was the nearest to making a first step toward peace that either of them had ever made in their lives. They couldn't understand how any man could be so plumb hostile and mean as to back-talk them after that fashion. Well, it took the wind out of my sails, too.

"I'm gonna go back and smash him," said Jimmy Clarges.

"Hold on, Jimmy. He ain't big enough for you to hit," said Soapy.

"No," Jimmy said. "He ain't a man. He's an insect."

"I'll tell you what I'll do," Soapy stated. "I'll get at him in another way. I see the way that I can hurt him most. Lemme talk it over with the kid."

He stepped aside with me.

"Kid," he said, "I've got the great idea for fixing that ornery Shorty."

"What is it?" I asked.

"I'm gonna sashay in and cut him out with the girl," he explained. "What do you say to that?"

Well, I swallered a laugh. Anybody that watched Rosita talking and smiling and blushing, would have figgered that she was pretty strong for Shorty. But it didn't seem to have sunk into the heart of big Soapy that way. He'd got a lot of attention that night, and I suppose he felt that he was pretty near invincible.

So I just said: "You go ahead, Soapy. But don't you get downhearted and mad if she don't pay no attention to you, because maybe Shorty has poisoned her mind against you."

"Maybe," he said. "But I dunno how a girl like her can waste time on a runt like him. I ask you personal and special, kid. Do you see how it could be?"

I kept a straight face, and I told him to go ahead and try his hand. Then I started looking for Jessica, feeling a lot better, because I allowed to myself that I had fixed things up pretty fine, and that there couldn't be no real trouble happen in the hall that evening. Which shows that I was a plain fool and didn't realize that the worst kind of tragedies start in with smiles, and not with guns talking.

Before I could get to my place, I was stopped by Jimmy Clarges. He said to me: "Hello, kid . . . wait a minute."

I stopped, kind of nervous, because I could see a whole flock of gents coming around Jessica.

He said: "I've got an idea for getting level with that kid, Shorty. I want to hear what you think of it."

"Fire away," I said, wondering what could be in the head of Jimmy. Because ordinarily he never bothered about thinking. He let Soapy do all of that hard work for him.

Jimmy said: "What put the hunch into my head was this. I seen what a fine, all-around looker the girl with Shorty is. And I says to myself . . . is he worthy of her? No, he ain't. Then why should he have her? He shouldn't. Then why shouldn't somebody else pry him away from her? Why, there ain't any good reason against that, is there? No, no good sense at all. And who's the man to be? Why, the first come, the first served. And opportunity, she never comes more'n once a day. Y'understand? Why shouldn't I go in there and try to cut him out?"

He wasn't quite as sure of himself as Soapy. But it amazed me to see that both of them had worked things out in the same way. No, it didn't amaze me none. Matter of fact, if you had one good look at the face of Rosita, you would have wanted to try just the same thing, and I suppose that there was a hundred men in that hall that would have liked to cut loose at her. But, when a girl gets to be just *so* pretty, she holds a gent back. Because you figger that some other gent must surely have the inside track—somebody a lot better and smarter and richer than you are. Y'understand how it is? It was that way with Rosita. There was nobody that bothered her much. Chiefly just Shorty that was always around her. And all the rest of the boys held right back. So Jimmy and big Soapy had both got the same idea.

"The finest chance in the world," I said. "You go ahead and win."

I might have said something better than that. I might have tried to persuade him not to make a fool of himself. But the fact was that I wanted to get rid of him quick, so that I could have a good laugh at him. I couldn't hold in no longer. So I sent Jimmy away to try his hand, and I sashayed on up to Jessica, who was just standing up on the floor with a gent, and the music was beginning with a bang and a whanging on the traps.

"Hey, Jessica," I said, "are you going to quit me on this here dance?"

"Oh," she said, blushing real hard, "that terrible program. I've just mixed everything up by losing it. Is this really your dance?"

"It ain't nothing else but," I said.

VII

There was a trail of black looks that followed me from the rest of those gents as I danced away with her.

"I'll tell you what," said the girl, "I don't think that this dance belonged to you at all."

"Well, sir," I said, "it sure does to the best of my memory, and a man can't do no better than that."

She looked straight and steady at me. "I think you have a *bad* memory," she said.

"I got one of the worst in the world, except about you," I said, "and I got such a good memory about you that I couldn't forget a single thing."

"You think that I'll believe that?" she queried, frowning. But she didn't mean the blackness of her look.

"I've got you all wrote down," I said, "from the color of your hair and your dimple to the size of your slippers."

"Well, I'll tell you what . . . a girl can't believe a single thing that you say."

"Hello!" I said. "And why not?"

"Because a girl hears you telling fibs to other men."

"Men don't count," I stated.

"Only the girl, I suppose?" she suggested.

"Not them, either. You're pretty near the first one that I ever talked to, Jessica."

"Kind of a wild and lonely life you've led, maybe?"

"Terrible," I said.

"In a wilderness," she said.

"Just about."

"And what did you learn to dance with?"

She nearly had me there, but that blessed drummer, he whanged the bass drum just then, and when the booming of it died away, I said: "You see, I was raised up with a mother and a lot of aunts, and such."

"Ah," says Jessica, "I'll believe that."

"Thanks," I stated.

"I've seen a lot of the boys learning to dance with their mothers and their aunts."

And she grinned up at me, and I grinned back at her. It was easy to see that she understood, and that I understood, and everything was pretty fine and happy. I couldn't help laughing. We swung around that floor like we was on skates.

"Look," said Jessica, all at once.

I looked. There was big Soapy stepping out with Rosita. Yes, sir, there he was as big as life, and with his fine red boots flashing, and his long sash tail flaring out behind him while he stepped away with Rosita.

I couldn't help staring. I really hadn't figured that he would be able to get a single dance with her, because somehow from a girl like that, you didn't think that she would let herself be made to look sort of funny dancing with a big lummox like that. But there she was, looking as contented as you could wish.

Then I took notice that Soapy didn't look so foolish, neither. I mean to say, he was wonderful light on his feet. You wouldn't expect that he would take such big strides around that he could hardly keep time. But he didn't. He come in with a click on every beat.

Rosita Alvarado was tall, too, which made the pair of them look all the better. And take it by and large, Soapy looked pretty gaudy, but not bad at all.

Well, I nearly twisted my head off my neck, looking at them. And so did everybody else in the room.

And then I said: "Where's Shorty?"

"Who do you mean?" said Jessica.

"I mean the gent that was dancing with her before."

"Jack Thomas?"

"Yes."

"Well," she said, "I don't know where. Gracious, I hope that he hasn't left the hall."

"Why? What do you mean?"

"What do I mean? Why, if he's left the hall, it means that he's angry because she's dancing with Soapy Almayer."

"What of that?" I asked her.

"Don't you know anything about Jack Thomas?" she asked me, leaning back in my arms, and frowning up at me.

"Not much," I told her.

"Well," she said, "there's a lot to know. If you was to go down into Arizona, maybe they would tell you quite a lot."

I said: "Thomas is a gunfighter?"

"Nothing but," said Jessica.

"How many has he got?" I asked.

"I've only heard of five men that he's killed," she responded. "Is Soapy Almayer a friend of yours?"

"He is," I said. "He sure is, and a white man, at that."

"Mostly," said Jessica, "I think that Jack Thomas has left the white men alone. He's done a lot of terrible things among Mexicans and Indians, but the white men . . . well, he's only killed five of them. But I don't suppose that there's anyone in this room foolish enough to want to make Thomas hostile." She added: "You look dizzy, Jim."

I took her over to a corner, and we sat down together.

"Tell me," I said, "is this Thomas really a bad one?"

"I don't know," she told me. "He's new on the range and in this part of the world, and we haven't heard very much about him. . . ."

"Just about the number of men that he says he's killed?"

"Oh, no," she said. "But there was a man who came through here from Arizona, and he saw Shorty Thomas, and he told what he knew about him. That's all."

Well, it made me pretty sick, as you maybe can imagine. I sat there and held my head in both my hands. And I thought that I could see the finish of the whole miserable business. I could understand why it was that Shorty had got into a rage when he'd been picked off his place on the bench that day in the camp. You couldn't expect a bang-up gunfighter that didn't fear anything in the world to take water even from a pair of giants like Soapy and Jimmy. What was size to him? The bigger the man, the bigger the target!

"What's wrong?" Jessica asked, and touched my arm.

Just then a gent came up and asked her for a dance. She only stared at me, very cut up.

"Go ahead and dance, Jessica," I told her. "I got trouble on my hands."

Well, off she sailed with that cowpuncher, but her glance was fixed back at me, and at any other time it would have pleased me a whole lot, the attention that she was paying to me,

y'understand? Just then, I was too worried to pay much heed to her and her nice ways.

Well, up comes Jimmy Clarges, just then, and he said to me, very black: "Say, d'you see what's happening?"

"Hello, Jimmy," I said. "What do you mean?"

"Soapy!" he said.

"Well?"

"He's double-crossed me."

"How come?"

"How come?" Jimmy asked, getting madder and madder. "Well, ain't he stepped in and cut me out with that girl?"

"Hello!" I said. "Is that the way of it? Look here, old-timer, what's he done?"

"He's dancing with her."

"Did you tell him that you wanted to stake her out?"

"Well, no."

"Then how d'you expect him to know what's going on in your mind?"

"He always knows everything that I'm thinking about," said Clarges, with a sigh. "He always knows. And he knows now."

"I wouldn't say so," I said. "You wait and think this over and give yourself a chance to cool off, old-timer, will you? You'll find out that Soapy didn't really mean no harm to you."

"I hope so," he replied. "I would take it pretty hard, to think that he would really have it in for me like that. Think of it, kid. In all these here years, we've never had no trouble with each other . . . not so much as one word of trouble."

"You won't have any now," I told him. "Why, old-timer, all that he means is just what you mean . . . to cut out Shorty with his girl."

Well, Jimmy was a pretty slow-headed fellow, as you can see for yourself. But now his face cleared.

"I guess you're right," he said. "Sure you're right. Old Soapy, he wouldn't try any tricks on me. But . . . wait a minute, kid, and tell me something."

"What's that?"

"Think it out for me. Now that he's danced with the girl first, have I got any right to ask her to dance with me afterward?"

Well, sir, it struck me all in a heap . . . it was so stupid, and so good-natured, and so faithful. More like the way that you would expect a favorite horse or a dog to think. I couldn't help liking Jimmy Clarges for it, even while it was hard to keep from busting out laughing at him.

"You go ahead and dance with her, if you can," I said to him. "I wouldn't worry about anything. Soapy, he's got a lot of sense. He wouldn't care. And if he did, you could smooth it out with him in two seconds."

"Are you sure?"

"Dead certain. Only . . . you won't be offended and make a lot of trouble if the girl can't dance with you? Because she's apt to have her program plumb full."

He said that he wouldn't, and that he would just take his chance on her liking him well enough to dance with him, and crowd him into a place on her program.

Well, sir, off he went, and I forgot the trouble that I was in about them long enough to see him rambling across the floor in the general direction of the place where Soapy was bringing the girl back, after the dance.

When I seen that, I ducked out of the dance room, and laughed all the way down the stairs. But, while I was laughing, I was looking, and I didn't see no sign of Shorty.

I went on outside, and there I looked up and down where the gents was standing around the horses, but there was still no sign of Jack Thomas.

"Partner," I said to an iron-faced cowpuncher that was leaning against a tree, smoking a cigarette. "Partner, tell me, did you ever hear of a gent by name of Jack Thomas?"

He gave me a side look. He was one of them slow kind that think before they speak, and then think again. "Some," he responded at last.

"You know him?"

"Some," he said.

"Have you seen him around here?"

"Yes," he said.

"Then where is he? Around the side of the courthouse?"

"No," he said.

"Maybe he's stepped across the street to where that hot dog stand is?" I suggested.

"No," he said.

"Well, where the devil *can* he be?" I insisted.

"Home," the iron-faced gent responded.

"Home?" I echoed.

He didn't say nothing.

"You seen him ride away from here?"

"Yes," he said.

"Thanks for the information," I said, a little peeved.

And I turned back into the courthouse again, more worried than ever by a whole pile. If he'd gone home that meant something, and it might mean something important.

I said to someone: "Did Thomas's boss send him home?"

"Thomas? Old man Alvarado ain't here."

"The foreman, then?"

"Foreman! Why, Thomas is the foreman, old-timer. Maybe he sent himself home."

And he busted out into a horse laugh.

VIII

Me, you can bet that I didn't laugh none. Not me! It turned out that Thomas was the foreman of the Alvarado place. Well, that meant that he was somebody of some importance, and not just a mere gunfighter, and that made things all the worse. You take a fellow with brains and get him mad at you, and it's twice as bad as if you was to get a mere ordinary fighter sore. Jack Thomas was mad. There was no sign of a doubt about that. He had gone home himself, and nobody had had the authority to send him. He had gone off and left somebody else to have the pleasure of taking Rosita home to her father's ranch.

Well, it made me feel pretty miserable. I didn't have the least doubt that Thomas had had a fight with Rosita, and that it was on account of big Soapy. And I didn't have the least doubt but that he'd gone off to plan how he could have revenge on Soapy.

And then, as I stepped into the dance hall again, I wondered to myself why it was that I had to do all of the worrying, and why couldn't somebody else take the affairs of Soapy and Clarges on their own shoulders? And wasn't Soapy and Clarges themselves men enough to handle their own things in their own way?

So, with the music blaring at me, and the slide trombones working overtime, I walked into the hall, and right away quick I found Jessica. And she found me, and smiled at me, like an electric light turned on in a dark room.

It wasn't no trouble at all to take her away from her crowd of gents and get the next dance.

"I've been terribly worried," she said.

"About what?"

"About you! Is there anything wrong?"

"Nothing much."

"There is, though. And don't tell me that you're going to have any trouble with that awful Jack Thomas."

I told her that I wasn't. And then we forgot ourselves and had just a plain, fine time dancing. But, as we pulled into the middle of the dance, I seen something more to give a man the

staggers. Yes, sir, right out there in the middle of the floor was Jimmy Clarges, dancing with his head throwed way back, and a grin on his face, and his eyes half closed, like he was so happy that he was drunk. And all around him there was a big empty space coming from folks having collided with Jimmy two or three times and getting wrecked, and realizing that it was foolish to let him jostle them. Nudging Jimmy was like nudging the shoulder of a granite boulder, he was that solid, and his idea of dancing was to go where his feet took him, regardless absolutely of how many other folks was standing in his way.

It was a scream to watch old Jimmy Clarges dancing, but that wasn't all. The girl he was dancing with was something. Yes, sir, maybe you have guessed it already, but the fact is that he was up there dancing with the queen of the mountains—Rosita Alvarado!

I looked at Jessica, and I asked her: "How come this, Jessica? How does it come that Rosita Alvarado is dancing with a big ham like Clarges?"

"Why," Jessica said, "a girl always likes to dance with a famous man, and Thunder and Lightning are both famous, aren't they?"

"I suppose they are," I agreed, but still I didn't think that it was enough of an answer.

"I'd dance with either of them myself," Jessica declared.

Well, she would, too, being a happy-go-lucky, free-swinging sort of a girl. But then she wasn't like that Rosita Alvarado. There wasn't anything queenly about her.

I finished off that dance, and hardly had a chance to get my girl seated when Soapy came up to me in a white heat.

"I guess you seen that? I guess you seen that?" he stammered at me, wild with rage.

"What in the world have I done to you, Soapy?" I asked.

"You? Who said that you had done nothing to me? It ain't

you, it's him."

"What him?"

"The low-life, wall-eyed, flat-footed skunk," Soapy hissed.

"Who you talking about?" I asked.

"I'll turn him inside out and see what makes him tick! I'll bust him in two!" Soapy stated angrily.

"You'll bust who?"

"He's double-crossed me."

"Who in the world do you mean, Soapy? Nobody would dare to double-cross you."

"You'd think he wouldn't dare," said Soapy, "him that I've taken care of like a baby all of these years, and worked over, and done his thinking for him, and slaved over him, and took care of him like he was a baby. But he ain't no baby, either. He's just a snake in the grass, I tell you."

Well, sir, I begun to see what he meant.

"Wait a minute, Soapy, are you talking about Clarges?"

"The rat-eyed, sneaking coyote!" Soapy snapped.

"Hold on, Soapy, tell me what he's done to you?"

"He took my girl," Soapy said. "Look at him over there now, grinning and gaping at her. He took her away from me. He sneaked in and grabbed her away from me, just because I'd told her some kind things about him, or otherwise she never would have wasted a second look on such a cow of a man. He ain't a man. He's an ox. No, he ain't an ox. An ox is too stupid to be mean. He's a. . . ."

I got more and more scared.

"Look here, old-timer," I said, "will you please listen to me?"

"Kid," he said, "you're the only one in the world that I *would* listen to. The rest of them are crooks and sneaks, but you, I'd listen to. Tell me what I can do to him, outside of just wringing his head off his shoulders for him?"

"Soapy, you're all wrong."

"I'm what?"

"You're wrong. Will you let me tell you what really happened?"

"Go on . . . go on."

"It was this way. When you started in to dance with Miss Alvarado, Jimmy Clarges, he just took it for granted that he should be able to dance with her, too. Like two brothers would go and dance with the same girl. And I'll bet that he ain't been doing a thing but telling her yarns about what a wonderful gent you are."

"Wait a minute," Soapy said. "That idea never came into my head."

He wasn't a fool, by any means, old Almayer. He was just pretty slow in the head.

"It's the straight of it, though," I told him. "Absolutely the straight of it."

"I believe you, dog-gone if I don't," he said. Then he gives a wriggle. "Look at him, though. Like a grinning baboon, and not like no man whatever."

Matter of fact, that was just about what Jimmy Clarges looked to be.

"Don't you worry none," I said. "He's tickled to death that you got him to know such a fine girl, but the last thing in the world that he would want would be to offend you, old-timer. I know him too well to expect that, and so do you, if you'd sober down and think it over for a minute. Why, old man, he loves you better than a brother. He's always looking up to you."

Soapy let out a few more breaths, and then gave a sigh. "I thought that I would have to break him up," he said. "And I been keeping myself from that all of these years."

"He's just a simple old chap," I said. "He don't think so fast and straight as you do, Soapy. You got to have patience with him. Otherwise, he would've asked your permission before he danced with her. She looked like she liked you a lot, Soapy."

"Would you say that?" he asked.

"Oh, yes. She was smiling all the time."

"Smiling, was she?" Soapy said, pretty contented. "Yes, I suppose she was." He waited for a minute, and then he added: "I got an invite out to her father's place."

"Go on, Soapy."

"I did, though."

"Old man, you're a fast worker," I told him. "The fact about her and Jimmy Clarges must be just that she took pity on him, him being a friend of yours, as she knew."

"Sure. I couldn't help mentioning his name a couple of times to her."

"It's all as clear as day. He don't mean any harm."

"I'll take it up with him," Soapy said.

That scared me.

"Don't you do it," I told him. "You just let the matter drop. I wouldn't say a word about it, if I was you. But I wonder at you, Soapy, the way that you get on with the girls."

"You seem to find yourself at home, kid," he said. "And she's a fine looker, too."

"Not in a class with your girl," I commented. "Hurry up and get another dance, big boy. We got to be starting back, pretty soon."

And away he went, with his head in the air, all smoothed out and happy again.

IX

It wouldn't have been hard for me to have laughed at the idea of those two big boobs that was wasting their time on nonsense, and in getting jealous of each other, while there was a hundred percent, sure-fire gunfighter waiting to murder 'em both.

What good would it have done to have warned them? No good at all. There wasn't any fear in them. And a fight against a gun would just be an old game for them. Many a time gents had yanked out Colts while arguing with Thunder or Lightning, and many a time the guns had been taken away and shoved down the throat of the gunfighter.

But there is men and men, and chiefly there is nothing much more different than an ordinary 'puncher, say, and a real gun-fighting fool.

I didn't need nobody to tell me that Jack Thomas was one of the last kind. He had the steady eye. And I'd seen him show his nerve. He wasn't the man to hold his fire until the last minute—and then miss the mark. Killing a man—if it came to that—would be no more to him than shooting a jack rabbit; he'd just be careful to pick his mark right. And what chance would the pair of the giants have against him?

Well, the rest of that evening went off in a dark haze, for me, with only a streak of light, now and then, where I seen the face of my girl. She was fine and kind and said I'd better go home and not stay here to be made miserable by something, she didn't know what. But I *had* to stay!

And a mighty good thing that I *did* stay, I can tell you, because in the finish there was a fine, large chance for a fight between that pair of hams. About 1:00 A.M., Rosita got up to leave, and who, I might ask you, was the gent that took her home?

No, you wouldn't really guess. But I'll tell you. It was Jimmy Clarges, with the floor grinding and screeching under his tread, as he went out with his head in the air.

Big Soapy leaned against the wall for a minute, pretty faint, and I hurried over to him. When he recovered, he made a wild lunge to follow them, but I hung onto him.

"Where you gonna go? Where you gonna go?" I kept asking him.

"I'm just gonna murder that sawed-off cartoon of a man," he told me.

"Wait, Soapy, and tell me what's the matter?"

He stopped dragging me toward the door, all at once. "No," he said, grave and sober as you please, "I ain't gonna spoil her clothes and her good time by splashing blood all over her. He ain't worth that much notice."

"You're right, Soapy," I told him.

"Sneaking in on me like that, the hound!"

"He's just doing it out of compliment to you, Soapy. I swear that's what he means by it."

Soapy gave me a queer look, with his forehead all wrinkling up, as much as to ask himself, was *I* mixed up in this here plot against his happiness?

But, in the meantime, what stuck in my crop, as they say, was the way that the girl had sashayed out of the room on the arm of Clarges, seeming as contented as could be, and smiling and chattering with Clarges.

Then I remembered she was a Mexican girl, and I thought to myself that there sure is something in the way of trouble in the air. There couldn't be any mistake about that! Something crooked was starting. Because, no matter what might be said about Clarges amusing her, she wouldn't let a big cartoon like him take her home! It wasn't possible.

Well, I was thinking things out like that while I hung onto the sleeve of Soapy and guided him, gradual, out of the dance hall. I told myself that if I could ever just get him safely back to the lumber camp without a fight, I would be thankful. How much he fought didn't make no difference to me, so long as he would just fight with the right man.

I got Soapy out of the hall and into the open. There was plenty of lights flashing, particularly the ones that come winking through the swinging doors of the saloons, where gents was filing in and out. And up in the hall, the orchestra was getting on its last legs and tearing off the roof with its closing pieces of the evening.

Soapy was sort of falling off and filling again, like a sail. Partly he wanted to get right on the trail of Clarges, and partly he wanted to get into one of the nearest saloons and pour down a gallon of firewater.

I knew what that would do. He would start in brooding over his wrongs and smash up half of the town. And how could I find a way for him to vent his feelings?

I thought of one, pretty soon. We walked by a sour-faced gent with a pair of shoulders almost as broad as Clarges's, and a nose squashed about flat with his cheek bones, and his eyes protected by a great, high ring of bone. He was a prize fighter, or had been one, and it was easy to see that there was still fight in him. He had a wicked light in his eye, for one thing, and he wasn't all bulged out of shape with fat the way that most of them get when they're out of the ring. I should have said that he weighed within ten or fifteen pounds of big Soapy Almayer, and all at once it come over me that the best thing in the world by way of preventing a tragedy was to get Soapy well beat up by that same ex-pug.

So I got away from Almayer and went back to the other gent.

"You're the Denver Kid, ain't you?" I asked.

"Me? Lord no," he replied. "I ain't that canvas-kissing sucker. Who says that I was? I'm Cyclone Charley."

And his eyes glinted at me. It was fine. He rose right up to my game like a trout flicking up to sock a fly on the surface of the water, not guessing that you got a hook in the fly. It was a pretty sight, I can tell you.

"Anyway," I continued, "I dropped back here to tell you that the big gent up there has got it in for you, Charley."

"Wait a minute while I catch my breath," Charley said with a sneer. "You pretty near scare me. What big gent? You don't mean that sap up yonder, do you?"

"Look here, Charley, I'm only warning you," I said. "The big guy says that you're a yellow hound, and that he dropped a lot of money betting on you, and that you quit, and that he's got a mind to run you out of town."

I thought that Cyclone Charley was gonna pass out. He wobbled a little, and then he lit out after Soapy, saying: "I'm gonna murder that poor stiff!"

I couldn't keep up with him. I didn't want to keep up with him. I just loafed along in the rear and laughed to myself. I'd played a sneaking part, sure enough, but just the same, though it was a shame to get Soapy beat up by a professional prize fighter, it would save him from doing worse harm before the night was over. Yes, I couldn't really blame myself.

I saw the prize fighter come up with Soapy, saw him tap Soapy's shoulder, and the next minute something was said between them, and I saw the big right arm of Almayer smash out like the lunge of a log in a jam.

Why, it was a pretty thing, I tell you, to see the pug duck that punch, and, coming up in close, he hit Soapy four times, with all his might, right in the stomach. It sounded sort of like the thudding of a drumstick on a great, big muffled drum.

I held my breath and waited for Soapy to go down, but he didn't go down. I seen his face by the light of a lamp that sent a streak out through a nearby window, and Almayer was just laughing and stepping in for more.

As he stepped, he punched, and the pug danced away before him, bobbing in and out among the driving fists, until he saw his chance, planted himself, and let Soapy have a straight right drive full on the button. Have you heard a cleaver go through a bone and chug down into the chopping block? That was the way it sounded. But Soapy didn't go down. Instead, he leaned in and reached the pug with an uppercut. It was just a half-arm punch. It lost part of its force by glancing off the chest of the prize fighter, but what was left of it hit Cyclone Charley on the chin, lifted him off his feet, and put him on the back of his head on the street.

He lay there without a quiver, completely done, and I came up and peered at him.

Soapy was saying: "You're a fine fighter, old-timer. Dog-gone me if you ain't a bang-up, real good one. Just stand up, and we'll have another round for the fun of it."

Cyclone Charley leaned up on his elbows. His eyes were pretty sick-looking.

"What happened?" he said, in a mumble. "Who hit me from behind?"

I dragged Soapy away. I was a good deal amazed. Mind you, I had heard a great deal about him and what he could do, but I never dreamed that any common man could stand up to a prize fighter. Well, neither could anyone. But Soapy simply wasn't common at all. He was about as uncommon as they come. He was plumb different. I couldn't understand how he had been able to weather those whacking punches to the stomach. But he *had* weathered them, and no mistake. He didn't seem to feel no aftereffect.

And it hadn't disabled him, that fight, but only it had cheered him up a great deal. He was smiling now and whistling as he went down the street with me.

"I feel pretty good, kid," he said to me. "I don't mean," he said apologetically, "about the fight, because it wasn't a real fight. But it was fun, y'understand? Because he wasn't too small to fight, was he?"

"No," I confirmed, "he wasn't."

"And he was fast, and a good, hard hitter," Soapy said, arguing with himself. "You got no idea how real hard he could hit.

He almost staggered me when he hit me on the jaw. And I think that he may've made a couple of marks on my stomach where he punched me. If only he could have taken it, we might've had a real, fine, upstanding fight, kid, and there ain't anything that does the heart much more good than that, is there?"

I said that perhaps there wasn't. And, while he was in that fine humor, I steered him past the last of the saloons and got him into the first buckboard that was starting back for the camp.

I felt that I had done a real good job. I was pretty pleased with myself. And, when the morning came, I figured that both Soapy and Jimmy Clarges would have forgot all about Rosita Alvarado.

That shows what a fool I am.

X

When I told the big boss about what had happened, he didn't seem excited none. You take most men, when they get along into middle age and when they've got their hands filled with power and with money and all that, they're so contented with their work and their own world that they don't care about the outside. And what's it to them if there's a man or two killed?

"There's maybe gonna be a dozen or so dead men around these diggings," I said to him.

"Let 'em drop, kid," he said. "Let 'em drop. I'm getting kind of tired of the dull life around here. In the old days, I used to be working with *men!*"

That irritated me a mite.

"You get off that old riot gun of yours, then," I said. "Because you're going to need it."

He looked at me a little more serious. That riot gun was an old-fashioned shotgun with two barrels, each like a separate cannon, and each barrel of it could hold a whole handful of loose shot. I had seen it, and I had heard a good deal about it and the way that the old man, several times, had downed a mob by turning loose on them with that terrible gun. His shoulder was layered with two inches of fat. That was the reason why he was the only man in the world that dared to fire the shotgun. It was sawed-off shot, so that the kick wasn't quite so great, now, and it was sure to dose about a hundred square yards of air with enough ammunition to blow a company of men to Kingdom Come.

"You think that there'll be a riot?" he said, pretty thoughtful.

"I dunno?" I responded. "If there is, I know that you'll enjoy it."

Of course, I didn't think that there was going to be any riot. To tell the truth, I was just leading up to something else. I was gonna tell about how the two big men was about to smash into each other, and then I was going to tell about the way that I had pried them apart from one another. I was just going to fix things up so that I would be admired a little. And maybe you understand what I mean—which is that after that job that I had worked on the evening before, I *needed* admiration. Maybe you've sometimes felt that way yourself. Admiring yourself ain't the same satisfaction at all.

However, I got away on the wrong foot with the chief, and so I went off in a huff and left him staring after me. And a little later in the morning, when I had a glimpse of him, dog-gone me if he wasn't working away and cleaning and oiling up the old riot gun and making her ready for action.

It sort of scared me. The gent who begins to holler—"Wolf! Wolf!"—out in a lumber camp is pretty apt to get all the wolf that he wants, and then some. Jostling lumberjacks is a lot more dangerous than jostling tins of soup.

Well, I had a man-size job lined up for me that morning, and, as I started away on it, I thought to myself that it would be a good thing if I should take one of the pair along with me.

Because that would keep them from any danger of mischief while I was away.

I got to Jimmy Clarges, therefore, and asked him to come along. "All right," he said, "as soon as Soapy is ready. He's down taking a plunge just now."

It gave me the shudders. A plunge, with the surface of the river along the banks all skimmed over with a glaze of thin ice! But that Almayer, he wouldn't hardly care for such a thing as that. He was like a buffalo. He would just smash through and take a frolic in the freezing water, and then come striding out and throw in somebody else that was standing and shivering on the bank. That was his idea of a joke!

Yes, sir, that very minute, there was a wild scream from down on the river, and Jimmy Clarges grinned, broad and slow.

"They're having their fun," he said. "And some more of it."

There was another sharp whoop, and somebody else must have been sent spinning into the water.

"Look here, Clarges," I said, "you better come along with me, because Soapy, he ain't ready to go, and I have to start off right now, and you're the only man in camp that's really got the strength to help me through with this here job."

"Not even Soapy?" he said, pricking up his ears.

"Not even Soapy," I said.

He didn't say a word. He just got up and followed me. Pretty soon, as we swung along through the trees, listening to the powdery fall of the snow from the branches now and then, he up and said: "A funny thing, kid, but. . . ."

"What?"

"You take Soapy, he's pretty big and grand, ain't he?"

"Sure he is," I said.

"Kind of a bull."

"Sure," I agreed.

"A bull moose, I mean," he said.

"Exactly."

"But there's some things that he couldn't manage."

"I got no doubt of that," I said.

"For instance . . . he's strong. Got a grand arm. Got fine hitting strength, y'understand? You ever see Soapy hit out?"

"Not really."

"You won't, either," he said, grinning and gaining in excitement. "Because, when Soapy hits, the other gent dies! He just dies!"

He made a pause. I thought it over, and I could believe it. I had seen the effect of a half-arm punch from Soapy on a strong man, a hardened, professional fighter. That little tap had flattened the pug as though a cart had driven over him.

"But I tell you what, kid," Clarges continued. "Maybe there's just one man in the world that could take one of Soapy's punches without being killed by it."

"Maybe," I said, sort of absent-minded and not exactly following what was being said.

"It would have to be a solid sort of a man," said Jimmy. "Somebody with plenty of underpinning, and built heavy and close to the ground, I should say. Wouldn't you?"

"Yes, I would," I agreed.

"But," he said, "d'you know anybody better fitted than me to fill just that part?"

"No, Jimmy, I sure don't. Did you ever take a punch from him?"

He shook his head. "Why, kid," he said, "we're both alive, ain't we?"

"Well, but men don't have to kill each other when they fight."

He stared at me, as though he couldn't understand why I didn't understand. "Him and me?" he said. "Soapy and me? Oh, if we ever fought, it would be killing. For both, most likely. Though maybe for only one. I'll tell you what . . . when we first seen each other, we both knew that, and we've never dared to touch each other ever since."

That was pretty frank talk. I had never heard Jimmy talk like that before, and gradually I began to wake up and see that he was hitting out in earnest and getting at something important. So I began to really listen and pay attention.

"I see," I said. "When I come to think of it, I suppose that if the two of you ever got smashing and crashing away at each other, there'd be two dead men."

"Maybe, maybe," he said.

He begun to whistle to himself, as he went along. It was just a thoughtful whistle from Jimmy Clarges, but from that pair of lungs and out of those lips of iron that whistling was like the screeching of a factory siren.

It was the right sort of a setting for the hearing of important talk, and I was getting it.

Jimmy said to me pretty soon: "I'll tell you what, kid. . . ."

"Well?"

"Speaking about how strong Soapy is . . . there's some ways where he's weak."

"It don't seem likely at all," I couldn't help replying to that idea.

"No, not to you, it don't seem likely at all, I got no doubt," he said.

"But it is?"

"It is."

"What way?"

"Here!" He held out his hands. His feet was no bigger than the feet of Soapy Almayer. But his hands, they was tremendous things.

"This is where he's weak," he said.

"I've seen him do a lot of queer things with his hands," I said. "I seen him break between his hands a board that couldn't

break over my knee." And, mind you, though I ain't a giant, I'm not exactly any man's weakling.

Jimmy just grinned at me and shrugged his shoulders. "Yes," he said finally, "he might be able to do that, too." But he didn't seem to be budged from his conviction. "I'll tell you the difference from his hands and mine," he went on. "He ain't got the size. And that means that he can't get the leverage. He just can't get it. He can bruise things. He can tear things. But I'll tell you, kid, that he can't slow and sure smash a thing, and turn it to pulp, and squash it gradual, and make the juice just sort of begin to leak and then to run and then to spurt out of it. . . ."

He was closing one of those big hands of his as he spoke, and I could see a man in that grip, I thought, fighting, getting weaker, sagging, and then his heart's blood spurting out. It wasn't a pleasant daydream, you take it from me.

"And suppose," said Jimmy Clarges, "that I was able to take one wallop from the big boy . . . and live through it . . . and get in close . . . and fasten a grip on him." He stopped. He stopped talking. He stopped walking. He stood and stared at his own idea. "Just suppose!" Jimmy exclaimed. "Just suppose!" And he licked his dry lips.

XI

Well, by this time I was scared, plenty. I knew something about the ways of fighting men, and I said to myself that if this wasn't a clear case of murder coming up, I would gladly eat the hats of the whole assembled crowd. I give Jimmy Clarges a hard, straight look in the eye, and he give me a hard, straight look back.

"Now, what's up, Jimmy?" I asked.

"What's up? Nothing," he said.

I asked him to look me in the eye. Well, he done it with the most surprising ease.

"Jimmy Clarges," I stated.

"Well, kid, what's biting you?" he asked.

"You're planning to murder Almayer."

"Murder? My God, no! All that I want to do is to beat him."

"Beat Almayer!" I shouted at him. "You're crazy!"

"Am I? Am I crazy when I say that?" he said. "Well, you wait and see, kid, and maybe you'll learn something."

"Maybe I will," I said. "Maybe I will . . . but why fight it out with Almayer, when you know that a fight with him is apt to mean a killing for one of you?"

"When things happen, they happen, and that's all that there is to it, kid," Jimmy Clarges pronounced.

"You've got to fight Soapy?"

"I got to." And he added suddenly: "Hand to hand, or knife, or . . . or axes, maybe." And he suddenly whirled his axe and turned it huge, double-size head into a streak of flashing light.

What a wrist he had! No, it wasn't a wrist. It was just a bar of steel. I thought that I might as well get some of his energy out of him. And I pointed out a big tree, and I told him to start.

He began with a shower of blows that ate into the rim of that tree wonderfully fast. But it was a big fellow, with a great, hard heart, and I guessed that it would take even Jimmy half a day to bring it down, because he never kept his axe sharp, and, in spite of all his strength, he didn't know where to place his blows to the best advantage.

I left him smashing away at that tree, and I turned back to camp.

The mail had just come up, and yonder was big Soapy sitting on a log and reading a letter. I remember that his sleeves was turned up to the elbow, and the big muscles rippled and bulged, and yet there didn't seem to be strength enough in him to keep that thin bit of paper from trembling up and down.

I went over to him quick, and, when he seen me coming, he grinned up at me, sort of foolish, and put the paper away. But not before I had a chance to see that it had feminine handwriting on it.

Soapy was getting a letter from a girl!

"Hello, Soapy," I said, "have you been busting the heart of some girl, you big ham?"

"Shut up, kid, you don't know nothing," he replied.

"All right," I said. "I don't know nothing, then. What do you know, Soapy?"

"Sit down, kid," he said.

I sat down on the log.

"Have you seen Jimmy around?"

"Jimmy's off somewhere in the woods working. I don't know where. Are you taking a day off, maybe?"

He didn't answer that. He just said: "Well, it's a funny thing about Jimmy. He's kind of deceiving."

"How?" I asked.

"You would think that he was too simple to double-cross anybody, wouldn't you?"

"Yes, and I think that he is."

"Well, that's what I thought. But I was wrong."

"I'd have to have that proved before I could believe what you say, Almayer."

"You would? I got the proof right here in this letter," Almayer said.

"Hey, Soapy," I said, "have you let some skirt get you all tangled up? Some rattle-headed, thick-witted, grinning fool. . . ."

"Hold on," Soapy said. "Is Rosita Alvarado any of all those things?"

Rosita Alvarado! And writing to big Soapy!

"What did she say?" I asked him.

"Say, kid, don't you think that I got no sense of honor?" he asked. "You think that I would go around and show her letter all over the world?"

"Maybe not. Maybe not," I responded.

I got up and went away. I was pretty thoughtful. It looked a cinch that Almayer and Clarges was gonna make trouble for one another, and the terrible idea come to me that maybe Rosita Alvarado had let herself get tangled up in this affair. I say it was a terrible idea, because what could she have to do with them, really, and what could they have to do with her? They was folks out of two different worlds. Even death and birth could hardly have separated them further, y'understand?

It didn't seem no ways possible, but all at once I decided that I would get at the truth under this here thing. I told the big boss that I wanted to go down to the town for the sake of clearing up something that had to do with Almayer and Clarges, and right away he told me to go ahead.

Ahead I went, and down to the town, as fast as a horse could gallop I got there. I got a change of horses at the hotel and burned up the road to the Alvarado house.

She wasn't home. No, sir, that beat all the luck in the world—for me to make as long a ride as that, and not to reach her in time at her house. Just plain, mean, ornery bad luck that was to have consequences later on, as you'll learn.

Rosita was over to the house of a neighbor.

I jumped for the saddle, and hitched the horse around and smashed away for the neighbor's house, and got there, and pretty soon I was saying to a Mexican servant all kinds of reasons why I had to see Miss Alvarado.

Then a tall, distinguished, old gent come along, and he asked what can he do for me, because he was the father of the friend of Miss Alvarado, and that talking with him would be just the same as talking with Miss Alvarado.

I listened to that bunk, and I thought that I would go mad.

Just how badly time was needed I didn't know, or how close Jimmy and Soapy was drawing together up there in the camp, but what I did guess was that every minute I really wasted might be fatal for somebody.

So I turned around when I heard the voice of a couple of girls in the patio beyond the room where I was standing. They didn't sound like the voices of servants, even though they was talking Spanish. They was light and gay and bubbling voices, and there was an easy sort of a something about them that made me feel that maybe this was what I wanted.

I said to the old gent that was chaperoning Miss Alvarado so careful that I thanked him very much, but that I thought that I could manage to help myself. Then I side-stepped through the doorway and glided right on out into the patio before the Mexican knew what I was about to do.

Well, he didn't have a fair chance to get heated up, because right there before me I seen girls walking arm in arm and chattering and nodding and laughing and bubbling like a pair of birds on the bough of a bush. It was a pretty sight to see, if you had any time at all, and I turned around, and I said to Miss Alvarado—sure, she was one of them—I said to her: "Ma'am, I got to take five minutes of your time."

Well, sir, that girl just passed a frosty eye over me and said to her friend—"This is very strange."—and turned her back on me and started to walk off.

She didn't walk far, though—because with one jump, I was in front of her.

They started back from me with a cry, the pair of them.

"Heavens, Rosita!" said the girl of the house. "What are we to do? Carlos! Miguel!"

"Lady," I said to her, "I'm sorry that I ain't got the time to be polite, but, if you start calling in a lot of your house *mozos*, this here place is all gonna get heated up and splashed with blood, I'm sorry to tell you. Y'understand? I got a reason for being here, or I wouldn't be bothering you at all, ladies."

They drew closer together and eyed me, but they didn't yap no more. A pair of sure-enough beauties they was, with eyes worth seeing, and their mouths more redder than you would believe of anything but paint.

I looked 'em over, and then I said: "*Señorita* Alvarado, I'm sorry to bother you, but I sure would take it kind if you was to give me a couple of minutes alone with you."

Her friend gasped and grabbed her arm, and Rosita Alvarado had plenty of nerve. I got to say that for her in the beginning and right away quick. She was as cool as you please.

She said: "Go over to the side of the garden, my dear. And I'll talk to this man."

Her friend hesitated a minute, and then she left and went over out of earshot.

"Now, what is it?" asked Rosita Alvarado. "And you do not know, I suppose, that it is dangerous to break into a house in this fashion?"

"Listen," I said, "I understand what your meaning is. You mean to give me a fair warning. But it don't bother me none. I've come down here to tell you about your dead men."

Well, it fair knocked her dizzy. She put a hand to her breast and closed her eyes.

"Not dead!" she gasped at once. "God forbid that they should be dead."

"What had they done to you," I said, "that you should want 'em to murder one another? What have they done to you? Answer me that!"

You see, I was fumbling in the dark, but it seemed that I had hit the truth nearer than I could have hoped. For now she cried out: "Nothing! Nothing! What were they to me? I was only to play the wretched joke for the sake of Jack Thomas!"

XII

There it was out of the bag. Jack Thomas—he'd used her to tangle up the pair of men that he hated. The little hound! The murdering little hound! I could hardly believe my ears. And yet there was an obvious reason for it. He couldn't use his guns on a pair of men who never carried weapons. And he couldn't be expected to stand up to them hand to hand. So what was he to do? Well, in a way it was a clever thing that he had managed. To make the pair of them fight one another.

"Joke?" I said to the girl. "It's a joke that you might have to answer for. D'you mind telling me what the joke was?"

"Why . . . it was only a little thing." She had to stop. She was trembling and almost crying. "I'll never let Jack Thomas come into my house again!" she cried.

"That won't bring dead man back to life," I told her, very stern.

Perhaps I was scaring her too much, but, after all, it was about time that she learned that the jokes a woman plays on men have to be of a certain kind. And better none at all.

"Dead men!" she sobbed. "Oh, oh, oh! But I tell you how it was. Jack Thomas had told me that the pair of them had bullied him in the camp, and that he wanted to get even with them . . . if only I would dance with them both and let one of them take me home. And then afterward, I would write a letter to the second one . . . but how could I dream that . . . ?"

"What did you say in that letter?"

"Oh, nothing worth repeating. Except that I was sorry that I had not seen more of him the other night, and that I hoped some other time he would come to see me and. . . ."

"And you asked Jimmy Clarges to come to see you, too?"

"Was that very wrong?"

"Was it wrong? Well," I couldn't help adding, "the fact is that neither of them is dead just yet, but, before I get back to the camp, one of them may be dead, or perhaps both of them. I don't know. I don't know! But if either of them starts a fight, the other one will finish it, and then you'll be to blame."

"But they're not dead . . . not either of them?"

"No," I admitted. "They're not."

"I thank heaven!"

"I'm sorry that I talked so mean to you," I said, by way of apologizing.

"It was a due punishment," she said. "And I don't complain to you. It was just and fair. I have no right to say that it was not. But, ah, how sick it makes me at heart to think . . . and they both seemed so simple and harmless and silly . . . how could they have killed anyone?"

I left her to think that problem out for herself, and tolerable, comfortable, because I knew that it would be a long time before she did any flirting with another man.

I wasn't in such a hurry to get back to the town. At least I was at the bottom of the affair by now. And it really didn't seem possible that those two big hulks would get to fighting just for the sake of a letter and an invitation to call. Well, that comes later.

As I was saying, I was drifting down the trail, easy, letting the pony take his time, and I remember whistling at a fool blackbird that would fly along and light on the fence posts ahead of me, from time to time, and, when he heard me whistle, he would flap his wings and skim over my head and land again farther up the fence line.

Altogether, I felt sort of relieved, though I couldn't tell why. Now that I had the clue to the whole thing, I'd simply go up to camp and tell the truth to the two big men. It was better for them to start in hating Shorty again than it was to have them hating one another. You can see that I had a pretty good reason for feeling comfortable about the thing. And I couldn't have

dreamed of what was really going to happen between them.

Anyway, there I was sauntering along, and taking it easy, and everything seemed hunky-dory, so far as I was concerned, and turning over in my mind the beauty of Rosita, and then harking away from her to what I felt was the cleaner face and the cleaner heart of Jessica. That was the girl for me! And while I was dreaming like that, I heard a clattering of hoofs.

I looked before me and seen that the pointed roofs of the town was just beginning to show above the trees. I looked behind me, and there was a rider sashaying down the road as fast as his bronco could lift him.

In another minute, I seen that it was Shorty Thomas, with the rim of his sombrero flared back from his forehead, so that I could make out his features very clear. It give me a terrible chill. The first thing that I noticed after that was that the flanks of his horse was all polished with sweat, and I figgered that maybe I could ride away and get to the town before him.

But a fine thing it would be to get to the ears of Jessica—I mean, how I had rode away full speed with Jack Thomas chasing me. It would make her laugh at me. And I couldn't stand for that.

No, my horse could possibly get me away from him, but I couldn't leave the trouble to my horse. I had to keep it for myself. And I didn't like the idea.

I was a fair shot with a rifle or with a revolver. Yes, I was a good deal better than a fair shot. And I don't mind saying that I could stand up to most men well enough with fists. But I never was any hand at making it a point of honor to be able to flash a revolver out of the holster like a streak of lightning. And I knew that was what Shorty could do.

I loosened up my revolver in its housing. And then I done the same by the rifle in the case that ran down under my right leg. And now, with the beats of that horse's hoofs rattling right in my ear, I seen that whatever I was to do, I had better do it right there and now.

I snaked that rifle out of the case, and, whirling my bronco around, I quickly jerked the rifle up to my shoulder.

Shorty Thomas, not twenty yards away, yelled to his horse, as he seen me halt mine, and he called out: "Hold on, Rankin, you low hound! I'm gonna. . . ."

And then the next thing he knew, I was tucking that rifle right under his chin. He hadn't expected anything like that, of course. He was a revolver man. That was his specialty. That was the specialty of all of those killers, you see? But this Thomas didn't lose his nerve because I had the drop on him, and his face, it was all wrinkled up with rage, something queer to see, and his eyes snapped and flashed at me. And he said: "You know why I'm here?"

"I can guess why you're here," I said.

"Because you stabbed me in the back!" he sang out.

"Because I've queered your game with a decent girl whose money you wanted. Is that it?" I suggested to him.

He snarled at me and got purple in the face. "Blast your heart," he said, "and put down that rifle, and we'll start on an even break."

"With Colts?"

"With anything that you want," he said. "I don't care what you use . . . but are you sure you have got the guts to make a fair and square stand-up fight of it?"

"No," I said, "I ain't. The fact is that I ain't a killer. I haven't spent six hours a day practicing with guns, the way that you have."

"You lie," Shorty said. "I never done that more'n half a dozen times in my life."

I almost laughed in his face. "But if you're just plain hankering after my life," I said, "I'll let you get out your own rifle, and

I'll let you bring it up to the ready . . . and, when you've got your gun at the ready, I'll bring mine back to that same position. And then you can try to drop me whenever you want, Shorty, because I'll be more than ready for you."

He stared at me very fixed and mean for a moment. "I think that you mean that," he said.

"You can place all your bets that I do," I said, and I looked him back in the eyes. Because, though I wasn't any blood hunter, still I was keen to hold up my end of this business, and, besides, I was getting a little hot under the collar myself.

Well, he looked at me for another minute, and then he said to me: "Rankin, it'd be no more'n a mutual murder."

"I don't mind dying," I said, "but I always have hated the idea of dying alone. You feel the same way, maybe?"

He showed me his teeth. He was like a bull terrier. Crazy to fight, but really with enough sense not to want to die. He twitched and fidgeted in the saddle, and half a dozen times I thought that he was going to take me up on my offer. But he didn't.

After a while, he said: "This ain't the only time that we're apt to meet, kid."

"I think it is," I said. "The gents in this part of the world know me, but they don't know you. They know that I'm not a bloodsucker, and they're beginning to guess that you're a scalp collector. And the fact is, partner, that, when I leave here, I'm gonna go straight to the sheriff's office and tell him that you're threatening my life. I think that maybe he'll ride you out of the county, after that."

"You yaller hound," he hissed. "You coward!"

"Drop all your guns and climb down to the ground, and I'll talk to you about that, too," I said.

Well, he sized me up, and working in a lumber camp most of my life hadn't made me exactly like an invalid. So the idea didn't look good to him.

"You better vamoose," I said to him. "We don't want your kind around here. You've missed your act with the girl and her money. And it'll be better all around for you to be carried down the drains before long. The world don't need you."

His nostrils flared and his eyes shot fire at me. And then he turned his horse around and rode off with no more talking.

Me, it left me pretty weak, and, when I got to town, I *did* go to the sheriff. Maybe that wasn't manly. But it looked safer. And I never hankered to be considered a hero. No, not particularly.

Reporting to the sheriff too, took some more time, and it had got terrible late before I headed me for the camp again.

XIII

I got to tell you now what happened while I was away from the camp, settling things with Shorty and Rosita Alvarado. You'll admit before I'm through that it was sort of queer that I couldn't have done things in time. It looked like hard luck all around. Fate, I would say.

Well, back from his job of woodcutting comes Jimmy Clarges with his pair of double axes on his shoulder, singing a song very gaily as he walked along. And there's a considerable snow blowing across the tops of the trees and settling pretty thick in the clearing around the camp, so that there was no chance of having lunch in the open air. The boys had gathered in the cook shack, where two long tables was laid out for them, and they come in stamping the snow off their shoes, and breathing steam out of their nostrils, and raring for chuck.

Things was going along fine in the bunkhouse, when in comes big Soapy and sits him down at the end of the table. "When do we stop getting beans every day in the week?" he shouted.

I have got to stop here to say that they was good beans,

though sort of frequent. They was done Mexican style by the cook, and some said that they was more Mexican than style to them. But I don't mind hot stuff.

However, nobody had ever heard Soapy—or Jimmy Clarges—growl about food in the camp before. Quantity, and not quality, was always what they was after.

The cook, he stands sort of petrified for a time, and then he sang out: "Him that don't like my cooking, let him step up and try to do better. Do I hear any answers? I don't! So shut up and feed your faces, and don't bother the only real working man in this here layout!"

You would figger that was talking up large and handsome to a gent like Soapy. And Soapy, he raised up on his hind legs and give the cook a mean look. But the cook was about fifty, and not much bigger than a minute, and so Soapy sagged back into his chair, too mad to eat and too mad to talk, and his eye roamed around the table like the eye of a mad bull.

And so his glance come to every man, and every man was looking down at his plate, very discreet. Because everybody knows that when a gent is mad, everything that everybody else does makes him just that much madder. Nobody stirred and nobody spoke, except one man, and he said: "I never ate after no better cook than ours. Take it easy, Soapy."

Soapy jerked up his head as though he couldn't believe his ears. And right down opposite him, at the far end of the table, he seen the head of Jimmy Clarges raise, and Jimmy looking straight at him.

"Them that ain't had no experience in decent food and cooking," said Soapy, "hadn't ought to criticize the complaints of them that have."

It wasn't much to say. Take it among rough gents like we all was in that camp, you might feel that it was hardly anything to say. But then, on the other hand, you got to consider who it was said to. Jimmy Clarges wasn't no ordinary man.

And now there was two general flashes of faces. One as all heads turned to Soapy, to wonder what had gotten into him, and the other, as all heads turned back to Jimmy Clarges, to wonder how he would take a paste in the face like this.

There wasn't long to doubt. Clarges shoved away his plate, and he bellowed: "I ain't had no experience? I was raised by a good Christian family, which is more'n you can brag about, Soapy Almayer!"

"There is some that has to brag to keep from bein' unnoticed," Soapy said very cutting. And he leaned back in his chair and smiled a little at the ceiling.

At that, Soapy could be plumb irritating when he wanted to.

"From bein' noticed by who?" Jimmy asked, sweating with meanness and bad temper.

"Whoever you please," Almayer replied.

"Not by girls, I hope you don't mean?" Clarges said.

"Hey, what's that?" bellowed Soapy.

"What I said! Some gets a minute of attention, but the longest stayer is the winner. The early bird catches the worm. You ain't the worm, by any chance, Soapy?"

It made Soapy turn purple. He knew that Clarges was bragging about having taken Rosita away from him the other night and taken her home after the dance was all over. And Soapy didn't like to think about that side of the affair.

"I have known gents," he said, "that never could get no attention at all, except from the folks that pitied them."

"Pitied who?" yelled Jimmy, getting hotter and hotter.

"If you ain't got no imagination," Soapy said, "why, kid, don't blame me for your lack of it. I ain't responsible for your brains. Go home and complain to your mamma and your papa."

It was getting sort of rough. Yes, even for a lumber camp. Particularly considering who Clarges and Soapy was.

Lunch was dying out. I mean, there was no particular attention being paid to the loading and the unloading of plates. The folks, they just sat around and stared at one another, and wondered when the lightning would strike.

Somehow the lunch, it come to an end, and after lunch, on these here cold days, the boys used to loaf around the fire and sort of steam out and take things easy, y'understand?

They did that today. Partly because they was in the habit, but more because they was bent on seeing what happened in this here quarrel. It was like a prize fight, but a terrible lot more exciting. Charley Fisher told me afterward that his heart begun racing and tearing, and his eyes swam. He near fainted before anything really happened—it was the terrible strain of waiting for the first jump of trouble.

"Where's the poker, somebody?" squeaked the cook.

"Here," Soapy Almayer said, and he took up the poker.

It was a big heavy iron bar, and the boys used to say that the little cook kept it more as a club than as a mere poker. Almayer took that poker, and he bent it double between his hands.

"There you are," he said. And he passed it to the cook.

"Hey, what's the main idea?" chirped the cook. "How can I really use a . . . ?"

"Wait a minute," Clarges said, and he took that poker, and just as easy as pie he unbent the folded iron again.

They say that you could hear the iron break in the terrible hands of Jimmy Clarges, and I believe it. Because I got that same poker hanging above my sitting room fireplace, right now, and there's the effect of the two bends in it, and the wrinkles of the fracture marks. It's hard to believe. I've seen two strong men try to do what both Clarges and Soapy managed, and the two strong men couldn't do a thing with that iron.

Then along comes the big boss. He had wind of everything in camp pretty quick, and somebody had told him that there was danger of something happening in the cook house. So he came over, remembering my warning and carrying his old riot gun tucked under his arm. And he come in muttering to somebody: "Where's Jim? Where's Jim Rankin? He's never around when I need him."

He used to leave most of these snarls among the men to me, to untangle them, and I used to have pretty good luck. Well, I wish that I had been there then, but I wasn't. The things had to happen that I could have stopped with two words, by showing that pair of great idiots that the girl and Shorty had simply been making fools of them.

I had no luck, and the big boss, he didn't know what to do. He looked at his watch. There was still ten minutes to go to 1:00 P.M., and he couldn't cut the lunch hour short by getting the boys out to work early. He thought of something else, and it was a good dodge.

"I haven't had a game of seven-up for a long time," he announced. "Who'll sit in with me for a little game? The whole gang of you, if you want. Soapy, sit here with me, will you? Chuck, start up a game over there. Take Clarges with you. . . ."

He had the boys in two parts, right away, and with something to think about besides the fight that was in the air.

"Hello, cook!" the boss shouted. "Got no better cards than these? These are no good!" He pushed back the first greasy pack, and the cook fumbled in his chest for some more.

"Maybe this pack'll do for the other table," Soapy said, slow and careful. And he picked up the pack of cards and drummed down the edges with his fingers until it was snug and fitted tight together, and then he picked it up and ripped that pack across.

Have you ever seen a man tear a pack of cards across? You try it with only a half of a pack and you'll see how hard it is.

He took that mangled pack and reached around him and laid it on the table in front of Jimmy Clarges. "Maybe that pack would be good enough for you and your gang, Clarges," he declared.

It was kind of a nasty remark, you'll admit.

"Pay attention to the game, boys!" the boss yipped, getting more and more nervous. "Hey, Soapy, it's your deal!"

He passed a fine, new pack to Soapy, but just then we saw Clarges take the torn halves of that pack and put them together, neat and snug, and then tear the two halves across, just as easy as Soapy had torn it when it lay single.

No, you would have to see if you would believe. But I got some of those cards. There was a great scramble for them, afterward. But I got a few in my possession now, and you can see where they was ripped across in quarters.

He turned around, and he said: "Here's four packs in exchange for your two, Soapy." And he laid the fragments on the table right before Soapy.

Almayer stared at them for a moment. He couldn't do anything better than this trick. He must have guessed at the full strength of Jimmy for the first time, and it made his face black as he stared. Then he jumped up and threw the cards in the face of Jimmy.

"You got no brains even in your insults, Clarges!" he shouted.

XIV

Of course, that was a lot more than enough. That room was instantly filled with diving men—some plunging for the door, and some for the walls, and some making the mistake of crawling under the tables. Because, though those tables were huge, heavy affairs, with the tops made of half logs, the inside surface planed down smooth and scrubbed white, they were knocked here and there and turned over as Clarges and Soapy got to each other and began to wrestle around.

Clarges had swung around from the bench he was sitting on

and rushed Soapy, head down, and his forearms curled up over his face to protect him from a punch.

It must have been that he had long planned just what he would do if ever he had to fight Soapy Almayer. And it was a good thing for him that he had, because the very first punch that Soapy used was hard enough to have killed a bull. It whipped straight as a dye for its mark, but, instead of the face of Jimmy, it reached the huge, thick cushioning muscles of his forearms.

Clarges wasn't hurt, but the terrible weight of that blow stopped him and straightened him. However, before Soapy could hit again, Clarges had fallen in on him and grappled him with his hands.

And after that it was another story.

Just as Clarges had said to me before, that same day, Soapy could really hit harder than any man in the world. But as for wrestling and rough-housing there was nobody like Jimmy Clarges.

The minute he got his grip, the gents, who was cowering under the tables and against the walls, heard a groan of surprise and fear and pain from the throat of Almayer. I suppose it was as though a bear had tackled him by surprise.

They began to thrash around here and there. Once, Almayer was wrestled down to his knees, but he come up again, lifting Jimmy with him, and turning both the tables upside down as he staggered back and forth.

There was plenty of noise, the gents shouting and hollering for fear they'd be stamped to death, as though by a pair of great buffalo bulls, and the big boss shouting for the two to stop fighting.

Might as well have called to the thunder and lightning for which they'd been nicknamed.

And then there was a whirl, and a gasp, and Almayer crashed

down to the floor with Clarges clinging to him, and crushing the life out of him with his long gorilla arms.

But still Soapy wasn't done.

The gents heard Clarges hiss: "Give up! Say you got enough, or . . . I'll kill you, Soapy!"

"Kill . . . and be . . . cursed!" gasped Soapy. And then his voice ended in a gurgle, because one of those hands of Clarges had fastened on Almayer's throat.

It was only a matter of seconds, then. The muscles in the neck of Almayer was like great pillars of India rubber. But the fingers of Clarges could crush rock, almost. I've seen him take two stones and crumble one against the other with his grip!

I guess that desperation made Soapy a giant for an instant. He gave a heave and a twist like a bucking horse. He couldn't have thrown Jimmy clear of him, but he did start them both rolling head over heels, and they went through the doorway and crashed down the steps of the cook house and so out onto the ground. And there luck gave Almayer a chance, for the head of Jimmy hit the knuckle of an exposed root that stuck above the surface of the earth, and Clarges was stunned for a few seconds.

It was long enough for Almayer to get away and stand up, and his knees was buckling under him, and his face was purple, and his mouth was wide open, with the tongue hanging out. Another second, and he would have been a finished man in that grip of Clarges.

Almayer, he went staggering around fumbling at the air, still full of fight, but blind and almost done for. And in the meantime, Clarges was getting back his senses, and, swearing terrible, he began to get back onto his feet. His face was like the face of a bulldog, they told me, as he started for Almayer again.

I got to give the big boss the credit that, when he seen them ready to murder each other, he was the only man there that had the grit to rush in between them. And he was hollering to the rest of the boys to help him stop the fight while he dived at Clarges.

Clarges simply swung out with the back of his left hand, and the sweep of it knocked the big boss clean away from him and rolled him head over heels in the moss and mud and sawdust.

The next minute, with a roar, Clarges was at Soapy.

If he had got Soapy in the first rush, that would have been the end, but there was just enough sense in Almayer to get him away from that lunge, and, in the meantime, every second was clearing his head terribly fast. After all, he hadn't been stunned, and a man will have a clear head from choking as soon as his lungs get properly filled with air.

When Jimmy Clarges, snarling and foaming, whirled around and rushed again, Almayer was enough himself to do a beautiful side-step, and cuff Jimmy in the face with his fist. It wasn't more than enough to knock out an ordinary man, and, therefore, it didn't have any effect at all upon Clarges. He rushed on in for more—and he got it!

You see, fighting in that little, narrow cook house, Jimmy had had all the natural advantages that he could get out of his gorilla strength. But now they was in the open, with snow to make the ground slippery, and the long legs and the faster action of Soapy gave him almost as much of an edge as though he had wings to carry him around.

He simply floated away from Jimmy, and, when Clarges reached for him, a fist like an iron-shod battering ram hit Jimmy between the eyes and knocked him back against the trunk of a tree.

That one punch just drenched his face with blood. Every one of Almayer's knuckles, like a knob of steel, had bit through skin and flesh to the bone.

On came Clarges, covered up like a prize fighter, and trying his best to close in on Soapy, and around and around that clearing they had it out, the most awful fight that any two men ever had in this here world, by the accounts of it.

Twice Clarges got Almayer for a fingerhold, and twice Soapy twisted away like a flash—because he'd come to dread that grip worse than fire.

But, in the meantime, with Jimmy all doubled over, and his long, thick arms wrapped around his head, Almayer couldn't get in a finishing punch, though he was hitting hard enough to kill a man with every stroke.

And then it was that I come into the scene—just too late. I heard the shouting in the distance, and I whipped that tired pony I was riding and raised a gallop out of it, but, as I come through the trees, I seen them at it, and I knew that I'd just missed my time.

I threw myself out of the saddle with a screech and started toward them. That instant Clarges got in close again and laid a wrestler's hold on Soapy. But reaching out that way, he left his head unguarded, and Almayer, swaying his whole weight forward and up on his toes, smashed an uppercut that grazed the chest of Clarges and hit him flush on the button.

He walked backward, his huge arms flopping at his sides, and his head swinging on his neck like a pivot.

And Almayer leaped after him to give the finishing touch. If that punch landed, it would kill Jimmy, and I knew it. I managed to get in between and tackled Almayer around the knees. It stopped him a fraction of a second. He reached down and plucked me away by the nape of the neck, like a grown man picking up a baby. But, while I dangled in the air, I managed to yell at him: "It's all right! I got the truth! She's been making a fool out of you and him, too."

He let me drop, but he didn't go on after Jimmy. He didn't need to, for Jimmy had stumbled over a little ridge of snow and fallen flat. He didn't try to pick himself up. Matter of fact, he'd been knocked clean senseless by that punch and only by luck had managed to stay balanced on his feet.

I had Almayer by the hand in a minute, and I tugged him away, talking a blue streak to him, all of the time. And the big boss, he understood what he was to do, too. He didn't need no telling. I'll say that for him. He come with a rush, and him and some of the rest of the boys was working away over Jimmy to bring him back to life.

I had Soapy against a tree.

"It was Shorty. It was that skunk Shorty that planned the whole thing," I explained.

Soapy raised a hand to his throat. The skin and the flesh was all tore where the fingers of Clarges had gripped him, and the blood was running down onto his breast.

"Shorty?" he said. "Shorty?" And his eyes was glazed like a man full of dope.

"Shorty!" I repeated to him. "The gent that wanted to fight you, up here. The gent that was with Rosita Alvarado that night. He hated the pair of you and wanted to get even. So he went to the girl. He got her to be sweet to both of you, so's he could get the pair of you into trouble with each other."

Soapy took hold of me. He sat down on a stone, and he held me in front of him. "Now tell it to me over again," he said. He looked as though he would break me open like an orange, if he thought that I wasn't telling him the truth.

So I said the same thing over, and then over again, and I told him how I had rode down and had met the girl, and had talked to her, and had bluffed her into giving me a complete confession of what Shorty had tried to work through her. And gradually, as Soapy's wits cleared after the let-down from the fight, he seemed to understand, and his eye cleared, and suddenly he said: "Then I'll get Shorty."

"Shorty is tracking it out of this here county. He'll never be seen here again," I told the big chap.

"But then it wasn't the fault of Jimmy," said Almayer. "It wasn't his fault at all."

"No," I said, "nor yours."

"Then I wish to God," Soapy announced, "that I'd never knocked him down, because he ain't gonna ever forgive me."

"You done him no harm after you floored him," I said.

He patted my shoulder. "No, kid, thanks to you, I didn't. But don't you suppose that he would rather be dead than have been beaten, even by a pal like me? No, no, kid, the harm that's done today, there ain't no undoing of it, and I've lost a gent that was more than a brother to me."

XV

That idea seemed to bother Almayer a tremendous lot. And the first thing that he did was to jump up and go to find Jimmy Clarges. I went along, of course, but we found that Clarges was gone.

"He wouldn't even wait to have a bandage put over his face," said the big boss. "He just went stumbling along through the snow and away off among the trees."

"He'll come back," snapped the cook. "He'll come back when his belly gets empty enough. I know these big men. They're all babies. They're all babies."

I looked up to the face of Soapy, and it was very dark.

He said to me: "Kid, I ain't any good at this woodcraft stuff. Are you?"

"What do you mean, Soapy?"

"Can you follow a trail?"

"Why, nothing extra. What trail do you mean?"

"I mean the trail of Clarges."

"Ain't you done him enough harm for today?"

"Aye," he said, "and I have, and now I want to do him some good. Harm? Aye, I've done him enough harm now and enough to last me forever." His big hand fumbled at his throat, and he shuddered a little. "Will you go with me on the trail, kid?"

While he was talking, the snow was falling faster. The air was streaked and clouded with it, and the ground was growing deep with it.

"I'll do my best for you, old-timer," I stated. "But we'd better start pretty *pronto*, if we want to catch him . . . even with the snow falling like this."

"We'll start," he said. "Are you ready now?"

"Aye, I'm ready."

He lunged off ahead of me in the direction that some of the boys pointed out to us. And, as he went, he passed by one of his own huge axes leaning against a tree at the side of the clearing. He snatched that up, automatic, and strode along ahead.

Ordinarily it would have been hard to follow that trail. I mean, if it had hit out along any of the frequented paths out of the main diggings, but it didn't go that way. It was like the trail of a blind man, full of reels and staggers, and pushing straight ahead, until he seemed to have almost run into a tree or something, and then veering off to the side, but on the whole keeping to one pretty straight line away from the camp.

Big Almayer interpreted the things as he went along, and he would say: "He's blind with the punch that cut his forehead and swelled up his eyes. Those eyes must be pretty near closed by this time. And besides that, he's more blinded with shame than with pain. He don't care much whether he lives or dies, except that he's prayin' and hopin' against hope that heaven will give him a chance to get even with us, some way. Oh, ain't he hopin' that he will have me by the throat once more. And then nothing in the world will ever let me get away from him."

Well, I suppose that was a pretty fair picture of what might be going on through the brain of Jimmy Clarges, and it didn't encourage me to go none too cheerful along that trail, I may as well confess. No, I was pretty well scared out, as a matter of fact, and ready to quit at any time, but there was no quit about big Almayer. The idea of being afraid of anything, I suppose, never come into his head. But me, I would've a lot rather've hunted a panther bare-handed than to try to hunt a devil like Jimmy Clarges in his present humor. But I had to go along.

It wasn't so hard to follow the trail, in spite of the fall of snow, because where Jimmy's feet had fallen, they had beat down the whole surface and made a great hole that half a day's snowing could hardly be expected to fill.

So we headed down that trail, with big Almayer following behind me, and breaking out into lively talk, now and then.

"Did he near have you, Soapy?" I asked him.

"Near?" Soapy said. "It was the nearest thing that you ever heard of, kid. The very nearest thing that you ever heard of! I was within about a second of dying. And then by the grace of heaven his head hit against something. What was it that we hit when we rolled down the steps out of the cook house?"

"It was a root that stuck up out of the ground like a rock."

"Ah-ah-ah," groaned Soapy. "I've stumbled over that same root a dozen times, and cursed it. And how was I to guess that I would ever owe my life to it?" And he added: "What's next from here?"

For we'd followed the path of Jimmy's big feet out of the trees, and into a broad trail where there was a jumble of tracks of men and horses and wheels that had churned up the snow here and beaten it down there. Several eight-horse teams had just been along that way, and it was pretty hard to make anything out of the jumble of signs. I was leaning over to study things out as well as I could.

But Soapy didn't hesitate. He struck right out ahead.

"Jimmy would head right on across this trail," he said. "He wouldn't be hankering to meet anybody on a road. Not the way that he's feeling just now. Not him. And the way that he's looking, too. No, he's gone on through the timber." And, with that, he headed away into the brush, and me picking up to hold after him.

But we didn't find the trail right away.

I figured that Almayer might be right, but that the snow over here might have been covering up the tracks, because now the trees were heaped with it, and the branches were bent and sagging and groaning with the weight.

We cut in a circle for a sign, and, finding none, we circled again. All at once, I grabbed the arm of Soapy. He stopped.

"What's that behind us?" I asked.

"Nothing," he said.

"I tell you I think that I heard something walking along behind us."

"What could be trailing us?"

"It ain't the first time that the hunters have been hunted."

"By a mountain lion, maybe?" Almayer said, grinning, and swinging his axe.

Why, sir, you could see that that big devil wouldn't have cared at all if a mountain lion *had* jumped him. With a blow of that axe he would have sunk the steel blade clean through a lion. I had to laugh, too, looking at him.

Just then, the wind freshened to a strong gale, for an instant. There was a crashing of snow all around us, and a groaning of trees already loaded with snow and now loaded twice more with the weight of the wind. A whole avalanche of snow hit the two of us, and left us gasping and blinded and laughing and cursing. And then, through the mist of flying snow ahead of me, I seen a great shadow falling, and a noise of branches whistling through the air, and the ground quivered with the shock.

I hardly sensed what had happened, at first, as I jumped backward. But then I guessed that it was the fall of a tree. And sure enough, there she lay full length—a real giant! The lightning had bit the trunk almost clean through the summer before, and the wind and the weight of the snow had done the rest just at that critical, unlucky moment.

There lay the tree, and where was Almayer?

I stared around, and then I heard a groaning, and I made him out, lying stretched on the ground, pinned down by a big branch. I shouted to him to get a cleat, and I grabbed his leg and pulled him.

Did you ever try to pull a two-hundred-and-fifty-pound man that was lodged in the snow, and caught in branches?

And just then the whole of that great branch sagged some more, and buried Almayer deeper in the snow.

He said, as clear as a bell: "I'm gone, kid. So long. It's gonna flatten me out. You better turn your back and. . . ." He stopped with a gasp of pain.

He was spread out helpless, and one leg was broke and bent back in under him, most awful to see.

Well, sir, I dunno what came over me—but the idea of that wonderful giant of a man being killed like that—well, it maddened me. I screamed like a hysterical woman.

And there was an answering roar right in my ear. It was Jimmy Clarges, charging out from the brush with the blackening blood still on his face, and his eyes purpled and closed. And I thought that he was just gonna kill me first so's there would be no witness, and then finish off big Soapy.

I was too paralyzed and scared to move an inch. And then he leaped past me and caught at the end of the branch that pinned Almayer down.

"I'll lift this," he said. "And you pull him out."

XVI

He heaved up on the branch. There was a shout of joy from Soapy, as he felt the weight taken from him, and he began to twist over and push himself clear with his arms, but, as he did so, some of the smaller branches of the tree that had been keeping the trunk from grinding clear down to the ground gave way, and the body of the tree settled with a shudder and a groan.

Almayer was pressed back into the snow and pinned harder than before!

It looked like the finish, you would say. And I stared across at Jimmy Clarges where he was holding up the bough. A weight that must have been tons had been throwed on him by the shifting of the weight of the tree. No, I suppose that I shouldn't say tons. But, anyway, I would bet that no one man ever held such a weight before, and no one will ever hold such a weight again.

He was drove down through the mud and the snow near knee-deep, to where his feet bit into the firm ground beneath. And then he could be sunk no farther. There he stuck, and he gritted his teeth, and his horrible-looking face swelled with the effort, and his lips curled back like a wolf's that's going to bite.

I watched him, like a man in a daze, and I heard him roar in a choked voice: "Get the axe, you fool, and chop off that branch!"

You see how complete my brain had stopped functioning.

I jumped for that axe and with it I ran at that bough. I had weighed and balanced the big axes of Jimmy and Soapy Almayer before that day, and I had wondered how any human being could manage to swing them. Well, sir, I was so excited and desperate, now, that that axe turned into a feather in my hands, and I flushed it almost to the wood with the very first stroke. I tugged it out, and then I began to hew away, and the chips flew out of that bough, just where it narrowed after leaving the trunk.

But, as I worked, though I was swinging that axe like lightning, it seemed to me that hours was passing, instead of seconds. And, though the chips ripped out of the heart of that bough faster than you could count, still it seemed to me that I was working in iron and not in wood—or just gnawing at that branch like a rat.

Because I could see two men dying before my eyes. What I mean is that Almayer was now crushed right against the earth, and the trunk of the tree was still settling. It was working its way down and down and biting deeper and deeper through the soft upper snow and soft mud, and eventually it would settle a whole foot or so lower than it was here. It was slipping gradually down, and, since Almayer couldn't be pushed any more in front of the branch, it stood to reason that the branch would push *through* him. Y'understand what I mean? And there he lay with his face turned up and going black.

And yonder at the end of the branch was Jimmy Clarges, doing such work as never was done before. He was keeping the weight of that branch; all that was killing Soapy was the settling of the branch itself. But Jimmy couldn't stand that strain any longer.

I seen his head thrusting up, and then sinking back and back, and the great cords of his throat, they stood out like so many arms.

"We'll save you, Soapy!" I screamed at him, slamming at the wood.

"You're doing fine, kid," he said, deep and quiet. "Don't you be afraid. I'm comin' out of this all OK."

"This here axe ain't . . . got . . . no weight!" I shouted, driving it into the tree with every word.

And then I heard a terrible cry from Jimmy Clarges: "Heaven, gimme strength!"

Seemed to me, when I glanced sidewise at him, that the

bough was eating through his shoulder and into his vitals, and I'll never forget the look on the face that he had turned up to the sky, nor the look of his hands as he gripped that branch with 'em, and used their strength to push upward, too. And as I looked, I seen the shirt split away over the swelling muscles of his upper arm and shoulder, and leave the arm naked. I seen that with one glance.

Then I heard a faint groan from Almayer, and I knew that nothing but death could have nudged that sound out of him. God put power into my arm, then. I turned and straddled the branch and give the back side of the limb two tremendous whacks. And the next instant there was a ripping and a splitting sound, and the branch busted off where I'd been cutting, and the whole trunk, relieved of that weight, rolled in a little mite.

But Almayer was saved, unless he had been crushed to death, already.

I looked out and saw Jimmy Clarges throw the branch away like it had been a toothpick, and him and me got to Soapy at the same time, and found him lying with his face swollen something awful, and his eyes fairly starting out of his head, and an awful grimace on his face.

I thought that it was the grin with which he had met death, but Jimmy had his ear already over Almayer's heart, and now he yelled: "It's beating, kid! It's beating! And he's living!"

He lived, right enough.

Soapy said, one day: "How could I have helped living, when so much had been done for the sake of me?"

He lived. I run all the way back to camp and got the big boss, who was quite a doctor, and he come back with me, and put the splints on Soapy's poor broken leg. And then a lot of us made a litter and carried Soapy back to the camp. And one end of the litter, the head end, was carried by Jimmy Clarges. And it was a wonderful thing to hear him and Soapy.

"How are you takin' it, Soapy?"

"I'm doing fine, Jimmy. Let somebody else pack that, will you?"

"Not me! Not me! I'm gonna leave nothin' concernin' you to anybody else, I tell you. We'll have you fixed like a king in a lot of down, old boy. Don't you do no doubting."

We did, too. We fixed up old Soapy fine. And he lay there in state while he was getting well, and lived on the cream of the land.

Somehow, the beating that Jimmy Clarges had got didn't seem to bother him none, after Soapy was brought in. But what we all thought was strange was that he would even talk about the fight. And he always underrated what he done, and how near he came to killing Almayer.

I heard him tell about the whole fight to a kid that was new to the camp.

"I managed to get him down with a grip on his throat," Jimmy said, "but he chucked me off him and through the cook house door, and, when I got up, he finished me with one punch. He ain't a man. He's a devil. Kid, he's the strongest man that ever lived."

Jimmy had stopped being proud of himself. He had just settled down to worshiping Almayer, and a good thing for Almayer that it was that way, for, though the leg healed, it left him lame, and, when the early spring weather come, we seen the last of Soapy and Jimmy walking away down the trail toward town, Soapy with a cane in one hand, and the other resting on the huge shoulder of Jimmy Clarges.

They was never heard of again, at least in these mountains. Thunder and Lightning turned into a legend. But I suppose that somewhere they settled down together in a quiet town, and by this day I suppose that Soapy is maybe doing some kind of office work. And Jimmy Clarges maybe is keeping the door. But together they have got to be till they die. Fate made them that way. They needed one another.

★ ★ ★ ★ ★

Legend of the Golden Coyote

★ ★ ★ ★ ★

While Faust often developed memorable relationships between humans and animals in his stories, he never wrote what one would call animal stories. "Legend of the Golden Coyote" is an exception in which the reader is introduced to the "golden coyote," members of his family, and a wide variety of animals living in the wild, all of whom commune with one another on a wide variety of subjects. The six parts of the story originally appeared as separate stories in Street & Smith's *Western Story Magazine* under the following titles: "Golden Coyote" (4/12/30), "White Hunger" (4/26/30), "Mother" (5/17/30), "Shivernose" (5/24/30), "Yellow Dog" (5/31/30), and "Back to His Own" (6/7/30). This is the first time they have been collected since their original publication.

I

When the light of the sun was yellow, and the sky turned blue, when the cañons filled with shadows like deep, translucent water, and the mesas drew away in violet mist, the mother coyote came out from the rocks with her tall son beside her. He was the color of the sun's light, so that she looked from the world about her to him and could not decide which was the more beautiful.

"Oh, my son," she said, "my golden boy, there are some who pray at the end of their work, but that is either to thank their God or to blame Him, whereas it is right that we should praise Him before He has rewarded us. Speak in this manner . . . Oh, God of the great and the small, who put under my paw the duck, the dove, and the snake, the frog, the mouse, and the rabbit, the sage hen, the calf, the colt, and the sheep, and made the coyote the lord of the world to read the wind and harvest the mountains and the plains, give to me this night not so much as I would have, but only what Your wisdom vouchsafes to me."

The golden coyote lifted his nose and wrinkled his eyes. "If I do not find wolf in the wind, my nose is blind," he said.

At this the hair lifted along the mother's back and she crouched a little. "Is it that mangy, big-footed fool from the river?" she asked.

The golden one thrust out his red tongue with laughter. "Perhaps it was only a fancy of mine," he admitted.

The mother shook her loose pelt until dust rose from it. "You are your father's son, entirely," she declared angrily. "If your heart were half as big as your great, lumbering body, or your spirit half as beautiful as your complexion, you would be a poet to whom every coyote would listen at moonrise, singing from the hills. But like him, you are a cynic, although I have told you a thousand times since your puppyhood that satire does not become you. What put that horrible thought of the wolf in your mind and on the long tip of your tongue?"

"You had just finished calling us the lords of the world," he said, "and I could not help wondering how long it would take me to make you shrink until your belly rubbed the dust."

At this, she stood tiptoe on stiffened legs. " 'They are wise who never hunted,' " she said.

"That is a maxim," he said, "but hardly a thought."

"Who are you," she demanded, "to talk of thoughts and of maxims? Have you ever killed so much as a stupid mountain grouse, or tasted a lamb of your own killing? You have broken the back of a one-legged frog that was asleep on the edge of the lake, and now you talk as loud as a grown dog."

"I am sorry," said the golden one, "but I really was wondering what made us the lords of the world."

"Very well," said the mother. "What is there under the sky that is greater than a coyote?"

"This same wolf that I spoke of," the son suggested.

"I will steal a sage hen out of the jaws of a wolf," she declared, "and carry it away so fast that the only thing he tastes will be my laughter. A wolf never looks well except when he is sitting down, as you know, or ought to know. He is a stupid, purblind glutton, cursed with an empty stomach, and never fast enough to fill it twice a year."

"There are the lynx and the mountain lion," said the golden coyote. "One of them could scratch our eyes out, and the other could break my back with a stroke of his paw."

"As for the lynx," she said, "I'll never deny that he has sharp teeth and a strong paw . . . but the poor starveling is like every other cat, a creeper and crawler that cannot range, and he trembles with joy if he can stalk a linnet and crush it under his big paw. As for the cougar, as our northern brothers call him . . . though he is rightly named the puma, as your uncle will tell you if you have wit enough to ask and patience enough to stop for an answer . . . he is still another cat and, therefore, really beneath contempt no matter how big he may grow. However, there is fat eating on the trail of a hunting mountain lion, and that I will not deny . . . but who would bless a spendthrift for the amount he throws away? Let me tell you, my child, that heaven is pleased by a thrifty spirit, and hates the wastrels like that same cougar of whom you asked. Besides, as everyone knows, the idiot thinks that he's a musician, and curdles the very wind and the rivers with his night concerts."

"At least," said the young coyote, "you'll admit that there is something to be said on behalf of the grizzly bear? I have never seen you cross one of those trails without turning about twice to ask the wind about him. He can tear down trees. And you have said that he is wise."

"The filthy thing wallows in mud," she answered, "and eats roots. Disgusting! I have seen him swallow a whole hive, bees, stings and all, so that my throat burned for a month merely to think of it. Concerning his wisdom, I don't deny that he is deep . . . but, for my part, I'm a practical person and never had any use for philosophers. What good is there in meat that flies over your head? In addition, he is so surly that one never can get him to speak out like a gentleman and a scholar, and, finally, he spends half his life asleep in a hole in the ground. Even the mole is more of a king than he at the time of his winter sleep. So I say again, the coyote is the lord of the world."

"There is that long-legged dog . . . ," began the son.

"Bah!" the mother cried, wrinkling her nose and sneezing. "You are disgusting. Every fool can talk, particularly young fools. Every dog is kicked by some man master and crawls back on his belly to be kicked again."

"This thing you call man," said the youngster, "I've never seen, but he must be a great thing, indeed."

At this, the mother yawned. "You are so young," she said, "that when I merely think of your ignorance, and of the distance you must travel in life, and of the burden of knowledge that I have to teach you, it wearies me beyond endurance. Particularly because, no matter what your natural talents, it is plain that you are no student. You are my son, and you may thank heaven for it . . . but, as I have told you before and now tell you again, a diligent fool may outlive the cleverest coyote in the world.

"As for this thing called man, you will laugh when you see him. He has only two legs like a bird, but, unlike a bird, he cannot fly. The poor wretch is born naked and has to cover himself with pelts that he steals from other creatures. He is so slow that even a squirrel can run away from him, and he is so dull that he could not smell a coyote at ten steps, or hear a fox at three. No, my son, there is nothing to compare with the coyote, and the older you grow the more you will be convinced of this truth, if you are spared from the trap. There is nothing in the world so fleet as the coyote except the jack rabbit, which we easily catch with a little patience, and the poor grass-eating antelope, on whose young you already have dined. We have sharp teeth to kill everything that we wish to eat, and whatever is too big for us to conquer we can easily escape. As for brains, we are a proverb for them both on the mountains and the plains!"

"You said something about a trap," said the golden coyote. "What may that be?"

"Great heavens," said the mother. "How green and young you are. This very minute we'll go to visit a trap, though I do wish that we had your uncle with us to teach you what he knows. And why do you sniff like that?"

"I don't want to hurt your feelings," said the golden coyote, "but it always has seemed to me that your brother is a mangy old bore. He has lost half his teeth, his eyes are continually watering, and he can hardly talk for scratching himself."

"Alas," said the mother, "you speak of the signs of age, and in the eyes of youth, to be old is to be sinful. Heaven forgive you, and make you remember that what your uncle is now, your own mother will be tomorrow. Now, come with me at once. If I talked to you until the stars came out, you would forget every word that I had said by the time the moon rose. No matter how long coyotes have lived in this world, each must learn again for himself with eye, and ear, and nose, and as for the wisdom of the ages, it never comes except with stiff joints."

After she had spoken in this manner, whining a little, she led the way from the rocks among which they slept in a small cave with three entrances, and, cutting across the hillsides, she dropped gradually into the heart of the valley.

It was now the rose of the evening, and, coming to a pool where the green images of poplars fell into a heaven of crimson and blue, she caught a frog and ate it on the shore, scrupulously leaving a half for her son.

"You see," she said as he swallowed his share, "that the Lord provides for the coyote even out of the waters, as from the dry land."

"Our cousin the wolf despises frog meat," observed the son, licking his lips as he finished a leg, having left the best for the last.

She smiled as she listened to the crunching of the slender bones.

"The wolf," she said, "is, in fact, a relative, but he is also a barbarian. No matter what airs he puts on, he never has been a true cosmopolite, and this is proved by nothing so much as his limited diet. There was a time when the whole wolf tribe ate nothing but buffalo, though how they could endure the boredom and monotony of that food I never could guess. Your truly cultivated person, my dear, is sure to have an educated palate. And what is education except the knowledge of many things?"

"That may all be very true," he said, "but, in the meantime, we are talking ourselves hungry faster than we are eating. Suppose we have a glance at the trap you were speaking of, although I would rather eat a good fat rabbit than do all the looking in the world, at the present moment."

" 'He who eats today may starve tomorrow,' " said the mother, who bristled with maxims more than a cactus with thorns, " 'and an empty stomach makes a sharp wit.' Now, let me see how you run uphill with no more than half a frog in your belly."

She set off at such a pace that he was gasping before they had gained the top of the next ridge.

"We're neither hunting nor hunted," he said, "and therefore why should we hurry?"

The mother did not speak, but one white gleam of her fangs made the youngster drop among the rocks at her side, his rear legs well parted so that his body could be pressed more tightly against the ground, his head glued to the rocks, also. She was in the same posture, and they restrained even their panting.

"What is it?" he gasped when he dared.

A shadow passed over them with a whisper, whereat he shrank yet closer, but it was only a great-winged owl that had floated down to look at these motionless forms, and sheered away when it discovered what they were. Yet the golden coyote stared after that form as it dipped into the hollow and out of sight beyond the next range of the hills, for it seemed to him a foreboder of ill.

By degrees, his mother raised her head. He imitated her, lagging a little behind, but as she did, half closing his eyes and working his nostrils, the better to judge of the wind.

"Now, little son," she said, "you have talked very bravely of many things, therefore, tell me what it is that comes to us here?"

Now that his opinion was asked, nine-tenths of his fear left him at once. He rose, sniffing.

"I have never smelled it before," he said, "but it is something that I would sooner see than anything I ever laid eyes on in my life."

"Would you follow it?"

"Whether it has claws or great teeth," he replied, "you have said that there is nothing from which we cannot escape. So I would go closer until I found it."

"You never would find it," she answered. "But, ah, that your uncle were here to tell you what it is. For that is a trap, my son. It has neither a body, nor hide, nor bone, but only teeth that bite out of the ground."

"Come closer," he said, stealing toward a bush from which the nameless fragrance seemed to issue. "Come closer, so that we can make sure that it has no face."

She flashed in front of him with bared teeth. "Ah, that I should have been cursed by bringing a fool into this beautiful and wonderful world," she said. "Go back, go back!"

He leaped sidewise, whirling to bolt, all his hair on end. It was not because of what she said, but because he saw a form arise from the bush before him.

Then a voice spoke, saying: "Which of my people are you?"

The mother had shrunk back, also, but, when she made out that this was merely another coyote, she regathered her courage and answered: "I keep a burrow among the Chantry Rocks. Who are you? I have heard your voice before."

"It is a wise coyote," he answered dryly, "that knows her

brother's voice."

"Ah," she said, "I have been wishing that I could have you here. My son is trap-mad . . . if only you would show him a lesson."

"I shall teach him with eye and nose," said the old coyote.

He moved, and there was a jingling of iron, so that the golden coyote slipped nearer and saw that about the foreleg of his uncle was fastened that same unbodied jaw of which his mother had spoken. To it hung a narrow chain.

"I shall bite the narrow thing in two," he said.

"Taste it, and try," said the other.

The golden coyote set his teeth on it until his jaws cracked, but he could not leave the dent of a tooth in it.

"You see," said the uncle, "that nothing is to be done. Unless, like a friend of mine, I chew off the imprisoned leg. However, the winters have been growing longer and hungrier for me of late years, and I do not care to limp through them on three legs. Moreover, this life is not all, unless the wisest of coyotes have lied to us, and I wish to stand on four feet before my Maker."

The golden coyote listened, dizzy with awe and fear, to the calm reasoning of the other.

"Is it fearful pain?" he asked. "Because the terrible teeth . . . they seem to sink right in."

"They are sinking in very slowly," replied the older coyote. "At first, it was difficult to endure it without howling. However, death will be still more difficult to bear, and that is soon coming upon me."

Pity overcame the golden coyote. "You say this because you do not know me," he said, "but I, the golden coyote, shall go hunting for you, and find the tenderest rabbits, the field mice, the squirrels, the frogs, and the ducks to bring up to you. After a time, perhaps, the pain will cease. You will live here pleasantly enough, and we shall come to keep you company and listen to your wise words."

The mother whined with sorrow and pleasure as she listened.

"What is the taste in your mouth?" asked the uncle.

"Something that I cannot describe."

"It is the taste of iron, and the hand of man has therefore been in your mouth. He has placed this trap in the ground. I, running downwind like a reckless fool, was caught here by my blindness and my speed."

"Alas, Brother," said the mother, "it is true that the swiftest foot is not always the first home."

The captive grunted. "You would moralize if you yourself were about to die. You will see, my son, that this trap was not placed here in vain. As you hunt for ground squirrels and rabbits, so man hunts for us. He will come soon with his fire-stick, and, when that speaks, we die. Go home. Keep the smell and the taste of iron in your mind, also the terrible fragrance of the trap. As for me, I am not sorry to die. I have lived a long life and a full life. Friends and enemies, I have given an eye for an eye and a tooth for a tooth. If I have been lean, sometimes, yet I have often been asleep with a full belly. If man kills me at last, yet he cannot take from me the memory of many a chicken, and goose, and colt, and calf, and sheep, and tender lamb with which I have comforted myself in winter and summer. I have lived a good life . . . I die without regrets. Farewell! Man is coming down the wind at this moment."

The golden coyote shrank back among the rocks and presently a black silhouette came over the hill's edge through the twilight and stood for a moment. Down the wind came the smell of iron, with a reeking new pungency about it. Then fire spat, the very ground seemed to shake beneath the young coyote, and he saw his uncle fall limply on his side. The red tongue lolled out. It was death.

Furtively, from rock to rock, mother and son scurried together down the slope into the valley, the golden coyote running ahead, unurged. When they saw lights before them, he would have stopped.

"It is the cave of man," he said.

"My brother is dead, and the hand of man has killed him," said the mother, "but for that very reason we should not shrink away from the vicinity of man. Rather, we should keep close, and see how we may steal from him. It is as great a glory to steal from man as to eat behind a cougar. He has dull eyes and ears, moreover, only there are the iron teeth that he leaves in the ground, and the fire-stick in his hand that makes us fear him."

"If God is just, why should He give such power to man?" asked the youngster.

"Because God is too merciful, and, when He saw the wretched, naked creature, without speed of foot, power of eye, strength of wit, cunning of nose, perhaps He was ashamed, and, therefore, He sent down iron to be man's servant."

After this, she led her son down to the farm. His heart was trembling with fear, with desire, with excitement, as they passed from place to place. She took him to the pig pens and showed him the beasts grunting in their sleep, bursting with fat. She showed him the long, white chicken house; he could remember the taste of the flesh that she had brought him in the days of his puppyhood, tender beyond belief, edible to the last bone! They glided through a hole in the barn, and the wings of pigeons fluttered in the loft. Sweet-breathing cattle munched the hay, and almost underfoot the little warm mice were scurrying. He pounced in the dark and found one with his teeth.

They went out again past the duck pond. They also had furnished tribute in the hungry days of his youth. In the sheep pens they saw the huddled fleeces, and the mother paused with lolling, dripping tongue, but went on again, for they heard a dog growl and turned themselves into furtive shadows that slunk away behind a shed.

Then the wise mother said: "The range is wide, but the range is hard. Your pads must become flint before you can run over it successfully. Here, after all, is the treasure house. It belongs to man, and everything that man has should be ours, for he has nothing except what he holds by the power of iron and not with the strength of tooth and paw. There is danger here, but there is also a rich mine of food. Many a strong coyote starves in the hills, but I, your mother, have never starved. Now come with me, and I shall show you the trap line that man keeps for us, and for the bobcat, the lynx, the wolf, and even the little rabbit."

They left the farm, and, drifting from the rich bottomlands, where the stars glittered deep in the breast of the river, they climbed the slope of the rocks. She picked the traps out, one by one, always with the same enchanting fragrance about them. Sometimes they lay in the open sand, where trails crossed; sometimes they were among the rocks, sometimes beneath a bush.

And the golden coyote studied with the most sensitive nose in the wide world the scent of the bait and the scent of the iron until he knew that his senses were attuned to them to the end of his days.

It was the intentness with which they mutually studied the trap line that almost brought them to disaster. But the mother heard a slight grinding of stones underfoot, on the slope above them, and her low yelp made her son look up in time.

Then the golden coyote saw two lofty silhouettes plunging toward him, two gaunt, long-legged forms of the hunting dogs of man. One was the shaggy-haired deerhound that his mother had pointed out to him on a day long before. The other was slighter, swifter of foot, bounding with a longer stride, and with a slick pelt, smooth as that of a wildcat in the spring of the year.

He fled at his mother's heels, his hindquarters doubling under him in the frantic effort of his gallop.

He would have turned down the slope, but his wise mother turned up against it, though that maneuver brought the dogs perilously close, so close that his pricked ears heard the hideous breathing of the monsters behind him.

Over the hilltop they fled into the face of the rising moon—a flaming torch held up to light the enemy's way. The golden coyote whimpered with dread, and shot down the slope beyond.

He saw the meaning of his mother's maneuver, then, for on the downgrade, the long legs of the hounds brought them up rapidly, though they lost ground again on the next hillside. Here the two fugitives ran well into the lead, but the effort almost cost the youngster the last of his wind.

His gallop broke as they passed the crest. "I am lost!" he sobbed, and turned down the valley beyond, keeping headlong to the downward slope, and sure as fate the two monsters swerved and followed him. They knew the weaker quarry!

A wise creature the golden coyote knew his mother to be, and a loving one, but he was amazed now to see her swerve back from her own course and, running as he had not dreamed even the arrow-swift rabbit could go, she crossed under the very noses of the dogs.

The teeth of the greyhound flashed as he leaped for her, but she doubled back under his very throat and he almost fell as he turned to follow. He had been played with, and maddened by that, even the youngster knew that the big dog would never leave that trail.

But the deerhound remained behind him, running with the same mighty stroke, its lolling tongue flashing in the moonlight. Twice the golden coyote tried to double back into the rough of the rocks, and twice it was headed and driven back downhill.

Numb from fetlock joint to shoulder and hip, half blind with labor and exhaustion, only the heart of the youngster kept strength. Behind him, he felt the shadow coming up, yet he dared not turn his head for fear of losing his stride. He dodged. Over him the great teeth flashed in a saber stroke and the big dog clumsily stopped and turned, for it expected the quarry to double straight back as a rabbit does. That was not the purpose in the desperate mind of the golden coyote. He merely had swerved, and now ran fairly past the nose of the standing hound, gaining wonderful distance in a moment.

In that instant of ecstasy, he told himself that the race was won, but almost immediately behind him he heard the dog coming with a whimpering grunt for every stride—coming up like the wind, with all its reserve strength flung into the effort. This was the run to make the kill, and the fugitive knew it well. He, too, found some meager remnant of nerve power to give to a last effort. His head wavered with his labor, and before him the lights of the house of the man appeared, blurred and jumbled by the movement of his head.

He made toward them blindly, not because it was the dwelling of man, but because it was an objective when nothing else loomed before him.

Dazzling bright those lights showed before him, presently, and he made for the open door as he would have made for any refuge. The very breath of the deerhound was at his rump as he bolted through into the scent of man, of steaming food that filled the air, of the heat of fire that throbbed in a massive thing of iron. There in the kitchen corner he whirled and heard the claws of the big dog scrape and grind on the floor as it strove to halt. A vast and shaggy monster, it stood before the coyote with red mouth agape and great fangs prepared for the final stroke.

Now the coyote heard a shrill voice that was man, yet smaller and sweeter than the voice of man, that ran in upon him. Even to his eye there was no danger in the girl who slipped to her knees beside him. Yet her hand struck the thrusting muzzle of the deerhound, and it recoiled. It came again from the side, and again the small hand threatened it away, so that now, in despair at this robbery, the monster backed away, and barked a protest.

"Look!" cried the girl. "Look at the dog that's come in, Daddy! Call Jerry away! Come look! He's all gold!"

The man came at that, striding huge and dark through the doorway, the smell of the iron about him, and the pungent death that had killed the uncle of the golden coyote.

"Dog, my foot!" he announced. "It's a sneakin' yaller coyote. Git away from it, Nelly, before it takes your hand off!"

He reached for her, and the golden coyote knew it was death that came near him. Death in the hand of the man, and salvation in the hand of the child. Around his neck she curled one arm, while the other hand gently stroked his face, covering his eyes with softness.

"He's not a coyote," she declared, "or if he is, he's as gentle as any dog. Call Jerry away. And look . . . he's all as golden as can be!"

The rough voice of the man answered: "The sneakin', treacherous, chicken-murderin' varmint! Git away from him, Nelly! He'd cut your throat as quick as a wink!"

The coyote heard. He did not need to know words in order to understand where the danger lay, and where the protector. From the fierce face of the man his glance was beaten away, but he looked up to the child and there for the first time met the eye of man and could endure it.

Voice, and hand, and eye had all one touch. The terror abated in him a little, and he licked the small hand beside his muzzle covertly, yet the man saw, and wondered.

"It's a coyote pup," he said, "growed into its size but not into its meanness. Look at old Jerry, there. Don't he know the breed, though? I'm gonna do this much for it. I'm gonna give it a start . . . it's surely got a second wind by now."

He called off the big hound and held it powerfully by the scruff of the neck in the door of the dining room.

"But I want it!" cried the child. "It's mine, because it came to me!"

"A pretty chance you'd have of keepin' it," declared her father. "And wouldn't it give your ma a turn to find a dirty coyote under the roof? Stand up, now, and watch it scoot."

She stood up obediently. The coyote rose with her, and pressed against her legs.

"Dog-gone me," said the father, "if I ever seen the like of that. Go to the door, Nelly, and see what it does."

She crossed to the door, the golden coyote sliding along beside her. There he saw the open face of the night, star-sprinkled, and bright with the moon; the wind blew all the familiar scent of the open world to his nostrils, and behind him was the terror of iron, of the dog, and of man.

But he looked up to the face of the child again. Her hand lay on his head softly, yet he felt the touch of a gentle mastery that was strange to him and strange to all his race.

Here the deerhound lunged furiously forward, and the coyote sprang unleashed into the dark.

He heard the tingling cry of the child's sorrow behind him, and then over his shoulder saw the hound streaking. All the peril was there behind him as before, but he had breathed; the fire no longer burned his lungs; his legs no longer sank beneath him.

He could not distance this enemy, he knew. In his young body there was no power to endure the long strain of the race, however, there were teeth of man's own planting in the ground, if only they would strike at the great enemy that sped behind.

Straight up the line of the traps he fled. A bobcat leaped up, with a jingle of the chain that hung from one imprisoned foot. It spat at him as he scurried by. And the deerhound went by with an anxious snarl, as though eager to take both quarries into its teeth at the same moment. Yet it clung steadfastly to the trail it was hunting under that bright moon.

Past a squat bush went the coyote, the smell of the bait whisking into its face, and the cold scent of the iron, then down into the hollow where the trap lay buried at the crossing of the trails. Right up to it he ran, until the tempting odor flared in his very face, then leaped forward as far as he could fling, landed, and rushed on untouched by the iron jaws.

Instantly, behind him, he heard the sound of a metal spring released, and then a dull champ as of teeth, and the rattling of the chain, and the shock of a heavy fall.

When he looked back, there lay the big deerhound with all four legs in the air. It stumbled to its feet, yet stood hobbled, with one imprisoned forepaw raised.

And the golden coyote sat down to watch.

Man and his works were mysterious indeed, but somehow it came into the mind of the young coyote that not all the servants of man obeyed his will implicitly. Some were friendly enemies, like the child in the house whose hand, as it were, still lay on his head. And yonder the dog was gripped by the bodiless jaws that man planted in the earth.

There was a frantic rattling of the chain, then a loud howl of pain, but the golden coyote arose, laughing, and trotted over the crest of the next hill. There he paused, and, scanning the plain beneath him, he sent his long, wavering cry into the moonshine, then waited with canted head.

He heard the mouse-colored coyote cry from the river bottom; he heard that old veteran of the Caspar Draw send up his pulsing wail, and last of all came the call of his mother around the very corner of the hill.

She met him as one rescued from the grave. She licked his muzzle; she whined her joy, and, when he took her back to the crest, she looked down on the prisoner and laughed a long, red laughter underneath the moon.

They killed a rabbit in the next hollow; they caught a sage hen only two hillsides away; they drank of the water that tumbles down the Caspar Rocks, and at last they lay before their own lair once more and looked across the valley, half drowned in the moon mist, but with the white mountain drawn wonderfully close.

"God has given us good hunting," said the mother, "and, more than that, He has taught you in a single night more than many a gray elder learns in a long life. For now I know what I guessed from the moment I watched your puppy days . . . you are destined to great things."

The golden coyote licked the blood from his paws and made no answer.

She continued, therefore: "We, who are both wise and brave, have watched man go by, close at hand, and studied his strange ways . . . but of all our race, you are the only one that has gone into his lair and come out with your life. Oh, my son, learn wisdom out of peril! And keep far from man till your pads are hard and your legs are strong. How else was I able to lose the greyhound in the rocks? The lumbering fool! Give me your promise now that you will never go back until I say the word."

But the golden coyote, his paws crossed at ease, had raised his head and was looking through the moon haze far off down the valley. Still he did not answer, and the mother murmured to herself: "How quickly they grow beyond us. How soon we ask, and they have the knowledge."

She dropped her head on her paws, and watched him askance, but the golden coyote lay like a statue and watched the moon slide down a western mountain like a great yellow wheel.

II

The oldest eagle that flew from the South Kendal Mountains could not remember a winter so long, so white, so iron-hard with cold. By November, Otter and Beaver Lakes could bear the weight of a walking man on their ice, and the Musquash creamed along its edges with freezing water. In December, all was ice except the cascade; the big trees of the Kendal Woods began to crack and boom like guns, and the Black Desert, to the south and west, disappeared under a gray mist of the snow that whirled in its continual winds. In January, even the cascade froze to a miracle of stalactites, and the golden coyote could run in the open or under the trees on the hard upper crust of the snow.

His fur grew long; the under wool multiplied; but still he was cold from dark to dawn and from dawn to dark of the short winter days, for continual, bitter starvation made him thin. It tucked up his belly; it arched his back; it reddened his eyes, and the robe that should have fitted with a tailored snugness over a layer of winter fat was far looser than the shaggy hide of a buffalo wolf. It moved in ripples along his back and over his shoulders as he ceaselessly tracked across his range. Like the heat of summer drought, so this cold burned him to the core and left him a mere framework of bones strung with tough muscle.

At least this winter made him learn his range from the South Kendal Mountains across the Musquash Valley to the North Kendal range beyond, and from the Black Desert to the dark, frozen shadows of the Kendal Woods in the northeast. He traveled and retraveled it, only avoiding the vicinity of the house and the barns of the man, which had been terrible to him since the dogs hunted him into the very den of the monster.

His hunger was a flame that burned without choice. He gnawed frozen moss; he chewed the lichens of wind-swept rocks; he wore his teeth on hard roots, and once he found a low-hung bat, sleeping its winter sleep. So he kept life in his body. He became all brain, all hate, all hunger. Since he had left his mother, he had not eaten once to his fill.

On this evening, as he came out of his den shivering, his breath smoking white about him, his tail curled between his legs, he saw the moon roll like a wheel over the gleaming edges of the eastern peaks, a broad-faced moon as warm and yellow as summer. The sight of it made him shudder more profoundly and lift his nose with a vain hope to study the air. There was no story of food upon it, but a disagreeable pungency, faint yet distinguishable, which told him that the great puma was already roving. He had seen the beast only the week before, with all its hair alert, its yellow eyes bent upon him with a dreadful affection.

This scent made the golden coyote tuck his tail still farther between his legs, and he trotted down from the hills toward the Musquash until he saw its glassy face shining, inhospitably hard. It was a treasure trove that the ice had rocked; it was a great storehouse of fish and frogs. On this alone an intelligent coyote, well-schooled as he had been, could live bountifully, but the key of winter had been turned and he was walled out.

By the first broad bend of the river he paused. Of the rock on which he and his mother had lain, fishing, only the glassy head appeared, slick with ice. When he came to the pool, he stopped again, and pushed hopelessly through the tangle of yellow reeds that bent above the snow. There was not a sound, there was not a sight. Here, where the frogs sang all the summer night, morsels of music more delicious to the tongue than to the ear.

He withdrew from the pool, and the changing wind blew clearly to him the scent of wood smoke and the odor of food poisoned with the smell of iron that meant man. The hair bristled along his back, yet, after a moment of thought, he knew that he would make the desperate adventure again, for he could remember mice, warmly burrowing in the hay of the barn, and chickens, sitting fat and stupid, wing to wing, along the perches of the hen house, and soft-throated swine in the pens, and cows in the shed, breathing out sweetness, with young veal somewhere nearby. All these memories suddenly maddened him. He went down the valley as though on wings, and still no sound or sign of life glinted to his eye from either hand. He went down the valley until he came to the hummock that overlooked the house of man.

What a change!

The barns, the sheds, the tangled fencing of the corrals, all were gone, and in their places remained only a black jungle of wreckage sticking its ends up through the snow. The house remained, with two windows watching him like great, yellow eyes. But the domain in which he was interested was gone completely.

He wandered through it. The gilding of ice had killed all scent except that of a fox, here, and a wolf, there. He was not the first hunter to prowl through the familiar place that had now been made so strange.

The courage of an empty belly, and curiosity, almost as strong in the golden coyote as hunger, sent him slipping and sneaking to the house. It was a riot of scents—of gunpowder, of iron and grease, which meant death; there was a rank scent of dogs, too, and of the man, and the child who had kept him from the dog on that unforgettable night when he had been hunted.

He reared, and, dropping his forepaws on the window's ledge, he looked inside.

Naturally he saw the dogs first, and at the first glimpse he stopped fearing them, and his mouth filled with a hot slaver.

They were not dangerous; they were food for him now. However the winter had treated him, it was killing the dogs. Their temples were sunken. They lay on the floor in a stupor, and, when they breathed, he could count the great outthrusting of the ribs. A touch of his bright teeth would finish them now.

The child lay in a bed beside the stove with round, open eyes that looked at the ceiling—eyes as stupid as those of the porcupine, which is too well armored to have either strong fear or strong wits. And the man, the great, strong hunter—he crossed the floor with sagging knees and leaned above the bed. His face was bones, breaking through the skin; the furrows in his cheeks had pulled back his lips into a horrible grin. He moved like a moose dying in the snow.

So the lips of the coyote curled in high fury and disdain. However, there was still the smell of the iron.

He would not waste time here. He only paused at the kitchen door to sniff softly, once. But the thousand odors of food all were old; there was no keen, living scent to inspire him so much as to wish to steal.

Up the valley he went again. Out of a clump of frozen brush arose a sharp-tailed grouse with a whir of rapidly beating wings. It passed him like a breath from heaven, just half an inch above the stroke of his teeth as he leaped. Its wings fanned warmth of fat blood into his face, and, as the coyote dropped, he saw beneath him something white as the snow and moving like a snake. It was tipped with black at the end of the tail. A weasel, and a bitter morsel in any case, but the golden coyote was desperate.

Down he dropped and struck for the back of the little destroyer's neck. He missed his mark and hit behind the shoulders, instead. The ribs crushed with the weight of his jaws, but the weasel had time to twist his head about and bury his snaky fangs in the cheek of the coyote.

The latter bounded back, tasting his own blood and that of the little white creature at once. He sat down to wait for the weasel to die. The stench was terrible. It poisoned the air. It was more horrible than the blinding medicine of the skunk, and no summer appetite could have made the golden coyote consider this thing as food. However, now this was a different matter, and he merely moved around to the windward side.

The weasel twisted in convulsions, but it talked as it died. "If I had found your throat, your throat," it said. "I could have drunk, and drunk, and drunk. Your soft throat through the wool, coyote! I would have locked my teeth under your jaws and tasted you living, and tasted you dead."

Sheer agony made the dying weasel chirp like a bird. He lay stretched out on his side, and the coyote moved a little closer, putting his head to one side to study his victim, but when he came too near, there was still a tremor of life in the ermine, and the golden coyote backed off in dread of another outburst of that putrid, that incandescent awfulness of stench. The ermine was dying fast, but it retained its malice to the last instant of its breath, gasping: "I have seen a mountain of meat! A mountain of meat!"

"Where?" asked the coyote, grinning with joy at the thought.

"A mountain of meat! A wapiti and a weak calf! A mountain of meat!"

"Where have you seen it?" asked the coyote. "Brave ermine, beautiful and white as the snow, where have you seen it?"

"A mountain of meat, a river of good, red, hot blood. A mountain of meat!" gasped the ermine.

Whether or not its information could have been wheedled from it, there was now a sudden hushing sound in the air overhead. The coyote flattened itself on its belly and threw up its teeth, only to see a pale ghost slide down on a sharp slant and strike a death scream from the ermine. Off it sailed on wide wings, a great white owl that had been driven so far south by what storms, or what freakish force of instinct?

It lighted on the top of a twelve-foot tree stump that had been broken off by a hurricane of the year before. The mother of the golden coyote herself had seen it fall. Now he slipped to the foot of the tree and looked up with fury and envy as the robber tore at his rightful prey. His belly worked with the very acid of hunger, as he saw the great owl consume the limp body in huge mouthfuls, swallowing hair and snapping bones in its powerful beak. The weasel was gone in an amazingly short time, and the owl mantled, then spun his head about to either side. At last it settled down with a ruffling of feathers and shrank in its head against its broad shoulders and blinked contentedly down at the golden coyote.

The coyote hated the very soul of the great bird, but he was not such a fool as to overlook a chance of gaining information from such an extensive and wise traveler.

"Father," he said, "you are welcome to my kill. I thank heaven that I have learned respect for my elders."

"And betters," snapped the owl. "If you're going to talk like a dove . . . how I wish I had one! . . . you might as well leave nothing out."

The coyote grinned with fury, but he controlled himself. "Of course," he said, "you know all the wisdom of the woods."

"And mountains," said the owl. "You kill like a fool," he went on. "But then, all you fellows who do your butchering by tooth are a clumsy lot. You have been so infernally slow with this white rat of an ermine that he's had time to douse himself with his musk, and I suppose I shall have a sour stomach for a week. My way, young man, is much better. They never hear me, and by the time they see the shadow of my wings sliding over them, I have them by the nape of the neck." He stretched forth one leg slowly, and expanded and contracted his great, wrinkled toes, shod with admirable talons. "They are dead before they have time to think," concluded the owl. "Accuracy, my lad, is what one needs in this harsh world. A good eye and an accurate claw will keep your belly full. But what is the use of revealing the truth to a born fool? I have seen a bear, now, do some very neat things in the way of fishing, and so forth. But you have no hands at all."

The coyote swallowed his gorge, though it nearly choked him to do so.

"Reverend Father," he said, "the sleekness of your feathers reveals like a clear pool the wisdom of your mind. And if I am not mistaken," he continued, eying a stain on the broad breast of the night hunter, "this is not your first meal tonight."

"I do not limit myself," said the owl, "to a meal of one course, like the poor, starved, four-footed beggars who run on the ground."

With this, he gaped and blinked rapidly. He could not have expressed his disdain more perfectly.

"You are, of course, the lord of the air," said the golden coyote, his mouth watering, his heart freezing with envy, "and your magnificent wings take you instantly to any food that you see with your beautiful yellow eyes."

"This light," answered the owl in its usual tart manner, "is much too full for you to appreciate the true beauty and brilliance of my eyes. They have been called," he went on complacently, "the twin moons of the dark forest, the golden moons, the moons of wisdom. Just to give you an idea."

"Father," said the coyote, "I hear you with wonder and admiration. To be beautiful is one thing. But to be both beautiful and a philosopher, and a poet as well. . . ."

"You haven't heard me sing," said the owl. "I have a range of more than four octaves. In my part of the world, where they know, the woods are silent when I sing."

"I have no doubt," said the coyote. "Your speaking voice gives me a slight hint, for, in a very modest way, I'm a musician myself."

"At least," said the owl, "I can see that you have a tongue in your head, though from the hollow look of your stomach, I have no doubt that your speech is wiser than your wit. Do you know where I can find me a few fat mice?"

"I shall put my mind on it," said the starving coyote, "and no doubt I shall be able to think of a good place. Of course, there is meat abroad. That ermine . . . the one you have just transferred to a warmer world . . . was telling me about a mountain of flesh . . . a wapiti and a certain stumbling calf. Perhaps your great eye has seen them, father, this very night?"

"Of course I have," said the owl. "I see everything. But it disgusts me to see great heaps of bones and flesh like that. What use are they, to creatures of any discrimination? I left them with hardly a glance and flew down the line of traps, yonder. There was nothing but one rabbit in them, however. But I thank heaven that it was not dead more than a minute and there was still some warmth in its blood. Delightful weather, isn't it?" he concluded, stretching out one wing, which was like a great soft white blanket, except at the transparent tips.

"Delightful," said the coyote, his teeth chattering. "The wapiti, father . . . you were saying that you saw them and. . . ."

"I didn't say where," said the owl. "I detest gossip. But at least I can let you know that I'm not facing them now."

"Ah?" said the coyote. And he looked away toward the tangle of the northern hills, a labyrinth at the owl's back in which the wisest of coyotes might hunt a month without finding the true trail.

"However, the mice, the mice!" snapped the owl impatiently, rising on tiptoes, its appetite apparently as fresh as ever. "Where are the mice, my young friend?"

"Just fly up the river to the second pond," said the coyote. "Among the grasses at its margin, I know of some of the most delicious mice in the world."

"I never despise information, no matter what the source," replied the owl, and, dipping off the tree stump, it sailed soundlessly off up the line of the river, never turning its great round head to one side or to the other.

The coyote looked after the marauder with a snarl. He had gained no useful information from that famous traveler, unless the suggestion about the trap line could be considered one. For his own part, not even famine had been able to draw him to the trap line, for in his youth he had learned enough about traps and their ways to last him the rest of his life. And sometimes at night he wakened, whining, from a dream of his wise uncle as he had seen that experienced coyote standing imprisoned by the trap. However, the taste of the ermine's blood was in his throat—the taste and not the comfort of eating; his bitten cheek stung him, and in a desperate mood he swung to the side and went up the wind with the smell of oil and iron momently stronger to lead him as with a light.

He found the traps one by one, stealing along, testing the ground lightly with each foot before he let down his weight, ready like a coiled spring to leap from danger. He came, at last, to a blur of red on the snow and a few trembling tufts of rabbit's fur. The coyote ate the blood-soaked snow gratefully. There was no substance in it, but at least it put a thought of comfort into his aching belly.

He went on, and came at length upon another trap that had been jerked from its hiding place. Its closed jaws were besmeared with clotted blood, and the forepaw of a coyote still hung in them.

Wolf, or mountain lion, or hideous wolverine, had come this way, perhaps. No, for a trail of red led swiftly from the trap, and away through the brush. He followed it. It was the trail of his own kind, but it is sad to state that the golden coyote looked upon cannibalism, at that moment, without horror. He did not so much as think of it, in fact. He simply knew that he was on the trail of blood, fresh blood!

The wind cut behind him. The fugitive had wit to travel down it. The telltale drops grew fewer and fewer, as though the cold were stanching the flow from the wound, but those few that the golden coyote found were ever fresher. He began to go blind with the rage of hunger, and wildly leaped a big log that crossed the trail.

A snarl sounded on the farther side. He whirled with greedy fury and saw the wounded coyote, with the footless leg drawn up and the hair bristling along its back. One leap and blow of his shoulder would knock it sprawling—and then the throat! Fear, however, seemed suddenly to have left the hurt one. Its humped back straightened; its hair smoothed; the glittering fangs were no longer bared.

"Oh, my son," said the voice of his mother. "I heard you on my trail. I thought . . . but the God of good coyotes brought you back to me."

The golden coyote crawled to her on his belly in shame and in pity. He sniffed the wound that her own cruel teeth had made. He rose and stood before her, shivering with cold and with fear of man. Even his wise mother had felt the iron teeth, in the end.

She seemed to forget her pain. "How tall you have grown," she said. "What a coat, what shoulders, and what a head. Except for your father's . . . may he rest in peace . . . I never saw a finer one!"

"I'm only a bag of bones," he told her, "and you seem to be little better. Have you no husband this winter?"

"I have had one husband, and that was enough," she snapped

rather sourly. "Besides, is this a winter to raise a family? No, I thank you. A fine thing, I must say, if I had little ones new and had to watch them die while I hobble, too lame to catch even a mouse. But as for me, I am old enough to die without mourning. I would have laid in the trap and waited for death to come, but I thought of man. And the smell of iron was horrible. So I set myself free."

He sniffed the clean cut that her teeth had made. Horror made him tremble. He thought of his own empty belly that all his wits and industry could not fill. But a great instinct rose in him.

"Come," he said. "You're a good deal more likely to die of mange and old age than of a missing foot. In the new of this very moon I saw a three-legged timber wolf as fat as butter and active as a marten. If such a slow-footed fool as a wolf can live on three legs, so can you. Yes, and even through such a winter. Besides, I shall hunt with you, and this moment we begin."

She licked his face tenderly. "I shall den up and sleep till moon set," she said. "And then between our wits we'll see what we can manage . . . our two wits, and your four legs, my son."

Into a soft drift of new-fallen snow they burrowed, and side-by-side they slept. It was she who waked the golden coyote, and they struggled out into the open.

The moon was on the edge of the western horizon, pale as a tuft of cloud, and a small sun, hardly more brilliant than the moon, was up to the eastward. In the door of their snow tunnel they lay and discussed their plans, while the son disclosed what he had learned the day before. On that, the mother decided to act. They should go back to the spot where he had left the white owl. She admitted that it might be difficult to find the reported elk and calf. "But any clue is a good clue," she said, "when the stomach is empty."

So they went down the valley. Her foreleg was inflamed and

swollen, but she paid no attention to it and ran with wonderful ease on only three supports, while the golden coyote looked at her with a smaller sense of having assumed a crushing burden. Her wisdom and his teeth might win the battle. He could guess at his added inches by the fact that she appeared so small to him now.

The day turned dark. The sun disappeared. Flurries of snow dropped from the sky like dusky birds. Then a pale form slid out from the trees beside the river and swept around above them.

"Liar! Mangy coyote, son of a farmyard dog, weak wit, and grass eater," hooted the angry owl. "There were no mice!"

The two coyotes sat down to enjoy this moment. "I told you where I had eaten mice," said the golden coyote, with satisfaction, "and where I shall eat them again in the spring of the year. Besides, I have eaten as many wapiti as you have mice."

The owl, with a whoop of rage, beat his great wings and shot away into the opposite covert to sleep for the day, perhaps.

The two coyotes laughed with red tongues at one another and ran on down the valley until a shrill, barking voice called to them from a hillside. They swung aside to come closer to red fox, a veteran of the Red Hills. He did not budge from them and their winter appetites, because he was standing at the entrance of a burrow that would be too small for them to follow him down to safety.

"He looks as fat as October," said the mother bitterly, "and he was born under a lucky star with that pinched muzzle of his, made to bite off the necks of fat geese in barnyards. Shall we talk to him?"

"He will make us angry," said the golden coyote, "but we may as well sharpen ourselves against his wit, if you please."

They stopped at a distance so close that the fox already was turning toward the entrance of the burrow. Now he faced them again, laughing.

"Good hunting, cousin," he said. "I see that you've made a good choice of company, for wisdom on three legs is better than a fool on four. Are you hunting for the mountain of meat, by any chance?"

"Have you seen it?" asked the golden coyote.

"Yes," said the fox.

"Brother," said the coyote politely, "such huge piles of flesh and bones are nothing to a delicate palate like yours, so you throw nothing away in telling us where the scent will be found."

The fox could not speak for an instant, since the wind, rising to almost hurricane force, staggered him, and parted the fur on his shoulder to the very skin. Then he said: "I tell you gladly that I saw the two elk between the Black Desert and the Kendal Woods. Hurry, my friends, before the gray wolves find and kill. I hear that you feed weasels to the owls to make them your friends, cousin?"

The golden coyote, overmastered with rage, had edged forward a little and now sprang like a cat, but his teeth clicked an inch from reynard's tail. Thrusting in head and shoulders, he was stopped from further progress, though he scratched frantically to push himself on.

The rankness of the fox's smell came up to him, and the ranker words of the wise hunter.

"You cannot grow a new leg, but you can at least grow new wits. Go back and sit in the snow and listen to the owls till you freeze. Go back! You will get nothing from me. Fools! Dog food!"

The golden coyote backed from the burrow and hurried off to join his mother, for he knew that he would gain nothing more from that poisonous tongue.

The mother stood up from a hummock on the lee of which she had been enjoying a comparative calm, but now she yelped through the howl of the gale: "We must go north of the

Musquash and trust to our eyes. Scents are frozen and fall to the ground, in such a gale."

So they went north over the Musquash River, and the golden coyote, ranging a little ahead so as to cover depressions and likely scenting spots to right and left, suddenly braced himself so sharply that he skidded across the polished crust of the snow. Luck at last had come. Bursting straight through the upper crust and driving down to the deepest layer of snow and ice above the surface of the ground, he saw the trail of the mountain of flesh!

Two had made the marks. The mother must have forged ahead, and the calf followed on the broken trail. So deep they sank and so sharp was the rim of the snow that it had sliced their legs, and the thin rims of red stain appeared every moment. The coyotes looked to one another. They neither howled nor whined. They asked not what strange fortune had driven the pair from their yarding grounds, but they fled down the trail in silence.

The wind was behind them, which would bring their scent before them to the elk, but that hardly mattered, since the big animals could never make successful speed across such going.

A mountain of flesh! Two mountains, but they would hardly be able to take the grown animal, with its dauntless courage and expert use of hoofs that could slash deeper than the bite of a bear or the rip of its claws.

The trail crossed the clear ice of a creek, and on that surface they could judge the size of the prints in spite of their sliding. A big cow and at least a well-grown calf.

The mother trailed behind, laboring with a pitching motion as her single foreleg grew exhausted by the strain, but, although she lagged, she kept doggedly at her task, while the golden coyote flew down the wind with hope making him light as a feather.

The gale fell away as swiftly as it had risen. It left the air wonderfully cold, but so still that the coyote grew hot with the labor of running. Down the valley, past the lower frog pond, skirting the arch of the river—what a fool was that mother elk not to take to the slippery ice!—and then, just above the house of man, turning sharply to the right, as though she smelled or saw the place for the first time.

That moment, also, the golden coyote saw the quarry, and for some reason out of his throat burst not the hunting yell but the morning song, smooth and musical as the cry of the loon. There was relief from famine with a vengeance, and salvation for all the worst of the winter that could remain. The cow was four or five hundred pounds of meat and bone on the hoofs; the calf was a great shambling creature, evidently late born, but all the more toothsome for that. Why ask for a mountain, when a hillock would be enough?

The golden coyote slavered with joy. Weariness left him. He could have ran all day, he felt, for such a glorious sight as this. But as he started forward again, the door of the house opened, and out came man, the hunter, with the gleam of a rifle in his hands.

The wapiti saw him, too, and started off at a run, throwing up clouds of snow dust. It was a close shot, however. And the coyote, seeing the man sink on one knee, for his own part guessed that the end was there. Had not his mother schooled him in the knowledge that even the swift and shifty coyote dare not give more than a running glimpse of himself to a marksman at three hundred yards? And this was a third of that distance.

The gun rang out. The golden coyote, stiff with despair and grief, looked sadly on, but the wapiti did not fall.

He could not believe what he beheld. Once more the gun steadied, yet not with the rock-like firmness that the golden coyote had seen in it before. Instead, the muzzle tipped and wavered. No wonder, when it spoke again, that the elk went on untouched over the rim of the next hill, and disappeared into the hollow beyond.

The man stood up, and, striking a hand against his face, he followed at a run. But what a run. So go the newly born, or the dying, with sagging legs. He tripped and fell full length. Slowly, slowly he gathered himself to his hands, to his knees, but the golden coyote waited to see no more. This great hunter would never come in gunshot of the wapiti again.

So he skirted to the right swiftly, and over his shoulder saw that his wise mother, traveling across the chord of the arc, was very close behind him. They rounded the hillside almost together, and could hear the crashing progress of the elk before they were seen striding up the farther slope.

The mother wapiti saw, also. She put on her best speed, but in the second little valley beyond she halted. The wind had kept the snow scoured thin here, so she began to trample swiftly in a circle that constantly enlarged, beating down the upper crust, making for herself a little pond, as it were, of loose snow and crusty fragment in which she and the calf could move with greater ease than even the light-footed coyotes.

But she had to stop the creation of that defense when the two prairie wolves came up and sat down on opposite sides of the circle, lolling their red tongues, waiting. Then she dropped her head over the back of the calf and glared from one side to the other, twitching her short stump of a tail, snorting, and stamping. The calf seemed quite unaware that mortal danger was near. It flopped its mulish long ears forward and extended its soft, bright nose to sniff at the coyotes. And the golden coyote laughed at his mother, and she, with red mouth, laughed back.

"I feint at the big one's haunch," she said. "You hamstring the calf, my son."

The whine scarcely had left her when she jumped straight

into the soft pulp of snow and broken crust and snapped toward the flank of the big mother. The elk half whirled, and the drive of the accurate forehoof barely skimmed the back of the prairie wolf as she squatted. Then back she jumped, wonderfully agile on her three legs. It was, altogether, not more than a second of play given to the golden coyote, but he used it to fling in behind the calf and slash with all the power of jaw, and wrenching head, and hard-tautened body, and the fear of death. Back he whirled as the calf bawled out in almost a human cry, and the big wapiti, kicking hard, skimmed her hoof along the flank of the young wolf.

Yet he was safe, now, on the rim of the snow.

"Did you reach the tendon?" asked the mother coyote.

"I reached it. I felt it jar and give under my teeth," said the son, "but I did not cut its whole breadth. However, see for yourself that it will not travel far."

Both the wapiti began to mill in a circle, the calf floundering and placing very little weight on the injured back leg. The crimson ran from it, a red promise of victory to the coyotes. The mother was frantic, yet she dared not charge the one coyote for fear the other would flick in at the calf. She could only shake her head and give her booming cry.

"We feast tonight," said the mother. "We feast, my son! Praise the God of all good coyotes! Sharpen your tooth for the next stroke!"

The big wapiti astonished them both, at this moment, by wheeling and, with a call to the calf, floundering away up the hillside. The youngling would have followed, but the golden coyote had missed once and he would not miss again. Under his flashing teeth he felt the tendon part with an audible jar above the hock, and the calf went down behind with a wild cry of terror and of pain.

Yet still the mother fled!

They had their explanation, then. For down the hillside behind them came a sound of crunching ice and to the nostrils of the coyotes the deadly odor of oil and iron. The man was there! Aye, running frantically, and now calling out, staggering, laughing like madness.

The coyotes ran for their lives!

And in the shelter of the frozen brush on the hilltop beyond, they saw the mother elk far away beneath them, on the open ice of the Champion River; they heard the clacking of her big, sharp-edged hoofs. She was far away, but more than that, she was off their range, and even starvation would hardly draw them over the mysterious borderline where traps might lie, who knew where? And where the air might drop, or the ground give forth what unknown dangers?

So they let her go, and lay panting, exhausted with disappointment, though they had been ready to run all day, not long before, with hope strengthening their legs.

"Heaven, who loves good coyotes," said the mother, much later in that day, "has left us our lives, at the least. Let us go back up the river. We may find mice."

They started back, but as they went a milder wind, a wind from the desert south, brought to them news of red meat. It came from the house of man, and, though they went without hope, yet still they went, until from the nearest brush they saw, cast out into the white arms of the snow, the spoils of the dead wapiti. Other creatures were there in the brush, crouching and starving—the same red fox from the Red Hills, panting with hunger, edging nervously away from the prairie wolves, and little crisp rustlings told of the flesh eaters nearby. They were watching the spoils, the great red blur of them from which man had taken what he wished. But above the house of man out rolled great volumes of smoke, and out of the house came laughter, hysterically loud, and now and then a white face was pressed to a window and looked out.

"Stay here, my son," said the mother. "Let me die if I must. But it is better to die with the taste of luscious blood in my mouth than with an empty throat."

Straightway she left the covert and slid out into the open, cunningly taking advantage of every depression until none was left. And behold! She stood at the food, and she ate, unharmed! Aye, though the white face of man gathered at the window and looked out.

The golden coyote sprang up, then flattened himself to his belly again, for he saw the great silhouette of the timber wolf skulking out toward the prey. There would be no room, surely, at the side of such a master.

A rifle clanged like two hammer faces meeting. The wolf, with a howl, wheeled and ran for the covert in such haste that the loose pelt heaved in waves above his shoulders. Mother coyote flattened herself in the snow.

Yet she did not flee, but with courage unprecedented she rose again, and she ate, and she was unharmed. Then famine turned the brain of the golden coyote. He, too, left the brush and dragged himself forward. He heard the dreadful voices of humans, but still he did not stop; death seemed a small thing to him, if it was not already lodged in his belly.

"Look! Look!" cried the voice of the girl. "It's the golden coyote himself! He's come. Daddy, don't shoot!"

"No," said the voice of the man. "Heaven bless him, tooth and claw. He could have my blood, if he wanted it. He's hunted for us all three, today."

The golden coyote heard. He did not understand, but he went on; he ate at his mother's side; he ate, and the wounded wolf howled to the sky from the dusky covert on the hillside.

Long after, they lay gorged in the den of the mother coyote.

"Listen, my son," said the mother. "It is evening. It is time for you to sing your song and give thanks. You can hear the puma in the valley, singing also to the God of the pumas. But our God is stronger. Praise Him and thank Him. For the God of the coyote stretches out His hand, and the earth is green, and mice squeak in the grass. He stretches out his hand, and the earth is white and hard as the iron of man. He stretches forth His hand, and man himself dares not strike. Man cuts the wolf with an invisible tooth and sends him howling, but when he aims at us, the strong God of the coyotes blinds him darker than night. Therefore, sing a beautiful hymn in his praise!"

The golden coyote yawned and showed every tooth in his long head.

"My belly is too full for music," he said. "But our God is good, and I shall thank Him in my dreams."

III

At the entrance to the cave, the golden coyote paused and looked back across the valley of the Musquash. Twice he canted his head to listen, and hushed his mother, who was panting up the hill behind him on her three legs. Most of the sound that welled across the slopes he could dissolve and trace to its sources—as the tremor and boom of the waterfall above Otter Lake, and the rapid chattering like human voices in dispute came from the cascade on the creek, while that rushing as of a wind through nearby trees was made by all the little rivulets that hurried down the hill to join the river. But he could not understand that which he heard only now and again from beyond the edge of the sky, sonorous but dim, like the calling of a moose. Sometimes it walked to him on the windless air from the north, and sometimes it seemed floating in the east.

"What is it?" he asked softly, at last.

"My son," said the mother, "it comes from beyond the Kendal Woods. It is the thunder of the Upper Musquash, rolling and shouting in its cañon. Once before I have heard it . . . it was the day of your father's death." She dropped to her stomach and began to lick the red from the white of her forelegs tenderly, with half-closed eyes, for they had killed young venison that evening. At last she looked up, panting, still lolling her red tongue. "It is an ominous sign," she said. "On that day I warned your father, but he would not listen. He went off, and he never returned. It was just such an evening, and the bald eagle of Mount Hope was fighting with a young stranger exactly as he is now."

The golden coyote had not seen. His look had been downward to the blue dusk of the evening in the valleys, and to the scent of young grass growing, and the taint of mossy trees. But now he glanced up to the heights of the mountains, still fingered with gold, and in the rosy upper air he saw the eagles fighting. Their dark forms seemed far too heavy to be supported by thin atmosphere, so that the golden coyote had a dizzy sense of looking not up, but down into water where two shadows were struggling. Soaring and stooping to strike, the great birds fought on the cold bosom of the sky straight overhead until their eerie screaming drifted to the ground. At last one of them dropped like a stone.

"He is dead," said the golden coyote.

"He is merely beaten," said the mother, as the falling eagle exploded its wings not a hundred yards from the ground and shot down the valley of the Musquash. The conqueror, wheeling once or twice to exult, then sailed away for Mount Hope. "He has won again," said the older coyote. "But one of these springs. . . ."

"Do they always fight in the spring? And why?" asked the golden coyote.

"Oh, some idiotic love affair, I suppose," she answered.

"Love?" said he gently. "What is love, Mother?"

"Love is stuff and nonsense!" she exclaimed with a start, and still as she spoke the skin twitched along her back. "And it's high time for you to go to bed."

"I'm not sleepy," he said. "The grass is cool here, and the air has a fresh taste."

"A damp bed gives rheumatism," she declared.

The son paid no attention, but went on with his thoughts. "Love . . . ," he said. "Is it love that is driving the world mad?"

"Love is madness," she said, "and of the most driveling sort. But what makes you say the world is topsy-turvy?"

"This morning," he said, "I saw a strange timber wolf come up the valley with the big gray monster from down the valley at her heels. She was young. She did not know the range, and kept turning her head from side to side. I stood close to the trail in some bushes, ready for the game when they should scent me and jump to get at me. . . ."

"Someday one of those games will cost you your throat," said the mother.

He continued slowly: "You would not have known the big wolf. He was thin. His tail was as high as mine, and his head was lifted. His eye was red. He had a foolish high trot, almost as stupid as that of a sheep dog. And both of them went by me as though I had not been there. That was madness, I thought. Then I went up the river, and saw the fox of the Red Hills fighting like fire with a stranger to this valley. The new fox won, and the old one went off, staggering, while a bitch fox came out of the brush and licked the wounds of this new chicken thief. That was madness, I thought.

"I went on into the woods. Everything was fighting, struggling, insane. I saw two squirrels fighting so hard that they fell off their branch and gave me a breakfast for nothing. I saw two badgers on the edge of the woods, holding one another, and tearing out fur and grunting like pigs. I saw the birds fighting in the trees, wrangling, scolding, and even the blue jay was serious for once and was trying to sing a song, which was so funny that I sat down and laughed at him. He usually has a sense of humor and nothing else but bad tricks, but, this morning, he went into a towering rage. He dropped to a lower branch and screamed insults at me and said my own song gave him colic pains and that I was the son of a yellow dog."

"The scoundrel!" exclaimed the mother loudly, jumping up, and then slowly lying down again. "The contemptible, gossiping . . . lying, I mean . . . rascal. I'll have his wicked head, for that."

"Oh, well, he can't help using his tongue. But I tell you, Mother, that it seems to me as though the world were on fire, for the mountains are smoking with water vapor . . . and the snow water is seeping through the forest mold . . . and the rivers are roaring like mad, shouting almost words, so that I found myself stopping, now and then, to listen. I swam the creek that runs down to the frog pond. I tell you that the current gripped me like the claws of a puma and pulled my head under. I came staggering up the bank, and a little weasel hissed under my nose, and then darted along after another of his kind. I am dizzy with this strangeness."

"It's the change of seasons," said the mother. "I'll take you to some excellent young watercress that I found today. There's nothing more cooling to the blood than a salad. Your father, who was really a connoisseur, always said so."

"I want to get out into the excitement," said the golden coyote, with a great sigh. "Listen! Everyone is out. The old grizzly is tearing out a bee's nest . . . do you hear the wood ripping under his claws? And there's the gray wolf howling . . . he's always off key."

"That comes from singing to an audience that's too large for him," said the mother. "Besides, he never had a sense of pitch. He strains to make effects, and that is the sign of the born fool."

"Hush," said the son. "Do you hear? Do you hear? Even the mice . . . they are scampering . . . they are rushing about in the grass . . . do you hear them? I am going for a walk, Mother."

"A walk indeed," she said. "A walk where? A walk to what?"

"Well, a frog, perhaps," he said.

"You've had enough to eat," she said. " 'Greed chokes puppy' . . . remember? . . . as your uncle loved to say . . . bless him. His conversation was a joy to me, my dear."

Overhead, a swallow dipped in the wind, and the faint cry came to the young coyote: "Love . . . oh, love." The bird sailed on to a twinkle in the dusk, and the word came faintly back: "Love. . . ."

The mother had not heard, but now settling herself in the most comfortable fashion, with her head up and her chin pointing high at the north star, she went on: " 'A glutton young, a beggar old' . . . your uncle used to say. 'Your eye is bigger than your belly,' he once said to your father. . . ."

The golden coyote recognized this mood, which was capable of pouring out proverbial wisdom by the hour. He slid to the side, putting down every foot with trembling care, and so melted into the darkness, while the voice of his mother continued blandly: "You've eaten enough for one day, my boy, unless you want to eat for the dog that will catch you. 'Are you fattening yourself for the market?' your uncle used to say when you were only a cub, too young to remember. Suppers killed more than all the doctors have cured, and temperance is the best medicine, my son. 'Light suppers make long days,' your uncle used to say to me, many a time, 'and a spare diet makes a sharp nose' . . . 'spare living and keen smelling,' he was fond of saying, for he was full of beautiful maxims, my dear. 'Go to bed without supper and you'll rise without debt.' "

Here her voice pitched upward in a scream: "My son, my son! Where have you . . . ?" She stopped.

The golden coyote was almost on the verge of running back to see what enemy had struck her, but he was still close enough to hear a light pulse of sound that he guessed to be her panting. He wondered, since she was so concerned, why she did not hurry after him—his scent lay plain to read upon the ground, but she did not stir, and presently he heard her whimper: "Oh, God of the coyotes, let him find happiness!"

He went on with excessive caution until he had reached the lower stretch of the slope, and then he ran on toward the frog pond, not that he particularly cared to go there, but because his own words to his mother had placed the pond in his mind. On the verge of the aspen grove, he heard a faint sound in the wet marshland, and with his paw he laid open the surface. It was a mole working rapidly; the prairie wolf took it by the soft scruff of his neck.

"Listen to me, worm-eater," he said.

"If you're going to kill me, kill me," snarled the mole in a tired voice, "but I haven't eaten a thing for five minutes, and another five will practically mean death by starvation. What do you want? You clumsy fool, stepping through the roof of a gentleman's house."

"After all," said the golden coyote, "you know the secrets under the ground. Or you ought to, because you live there. That was why I dug you up, because I wanted to know the opinion of such a great scholar as you. What is love, if you please?"

"My heaven," said the mole. "I am a delver into mysteries, and I have fallen into the hands of a gossip. Let me go. Unless you have a few good worms at hand. I cannot think without eating. . . ."

"Your answer," said the coyote, "or I'll break your neck."

"It turns my stomach to merely think of it," said the mole. "I hope that's answer enough. It's a subject that well-bred people have avoided for centuries. If it has to be, well, let us at least put it in a silent pocket or leave it for the doves and poets and fools to talk about."

The golden coyote was so annoyed that he could not help giving the mole's neck a pinch. Then he tossed the flabby creature aside, saying merely—"I hope your next grub chokes you."—and went on. "The doves," he said, "I must find them. I hope it is not too late."

The coyote ran with all his might. The small runlets flashed beneath his paws, gilded or red with the last of the day's light, and he came to the stream where the doves were dipping out of the dying sunset to drink, and to sit on a bough, to croon, and to fly again. He could hear them in the distance, like the humming of a great hive of bees, and, when he came closer, there were so many voices thronging the still air that he was amazed. He could hear no words, at first, but only the music of a hundred swelling throats that, as he studied it, seemed to change into one word alone: "Love, love, love. . . ."

The sound of it fascinated him; he grew a little dizzy, as he had been when he looked up at the two eagles fighting so far above him. For all of these voices sang alone, and yet all blended into one gentle harmony. He paused beneath a tree, and now he could hear the singer above him chanting in the most mournful fashion: "Oh, pain! Oh, sweet, sweet love!"

"Pardon me," said the golden coyote in his gentlest voice, "but can you tell me what this love is of which you speak?"

The dove paid not the slightest attention, but in exactly the same accent repeated: "Oh, pain! Oh, sweet, sweet love!"

The golden coyote went on to another tree, and there he heard two voices answering one another in a dialogue that was all song, intermingling, interrupting, blending together always.

"I came through the desert, for love carried me. Love was in the desert."

"I came from the north, following love. The birch trees stand like white spirits, in trembling clouds of green."

"Love is in the desert. There I found the little mimulus looking up at me with yellow eyes, and the baby blue eyes, sprinkled with black, even on the desert. In the dusk there are stars on the desert, the evening primrose opening."

"Love flew with me out of the north. The world is dissolving in the fire of love. The soft maples are smoking with green, and the red maples are clustered with bronze. The dust of love is falling from the willows."

"Love is crossing the desert like a sea, for I saw a lark and a bobolink, and a mocking bird and a linnet. They all flew north, but I alone have found you, oh, my love."

Then the golden coyote spoke, but they would not answer. He heard the whisper of their wings, and the two voices faded in the air.

"Love has come from the desert . . . love . . . from the . . . north. . . ."

The golden coyote sighed, and the sigh made him sneeze, which silenced every songster near at hand, but still, from high up the stream and below, the cooing continued and closed again over his head with music.

"I love, and I die for it. Pity me, mourn for me! Ah, loveliness and sorrow. . . ."

The golden coyote felt that he could stand it no longer. He was dizzier than ever, and, since not a one of these rhapsodists would answer him, he turned back and hurried toward the frog pond in desperate haste, for somehow he felt that he must be answered before the gray of the evening closed its hands over the central sky.

He pushed through the reeds. He stood fetlock-deep in the

slime and water at the edge of the pool. The frogs were silent. Only the rose and gold of the heavens lay on the water, and one dusky shadow. He had to study this in the face of the pool before he was able to see a great blue heron standing almost knee-deep on the other side of the narrow water, so deftly did its coloring blend with the twilight haze.

"Hush," said the heron, as soon as it saw that it was noticed.

"I beg your pardon," said the golden coyote, "but I must speak."

"Softly, then, if you please," said the heron. "The frogs are about to come out to sing, and I love their chorus in this valley. The echoes are so soft, so appetizingly delicate. What is it that you wish to ask me?"

"About love," said the coyote.

The heron was continually smiling, or had the look of it, with sardonic wrinkles around the top of its beak, but at this question it seemed about to laugh. It closed and reopened its bill several times, stretching its neck.

"I would have laughed, I confess," she said, "except that the last fish caught in my throat. Love, is it? My dear young fellow, what have you to do with love?"

"Why, the whole world is talking of nothing else!" exclaimed the coyote.

"I hope that I am a part of the world," said the heron, "and I assure you that I'm only talking about love to answer a question. I don't deny that I have a husband or two, but I hope to the wise God of the herons that I have outgrown the folly of that. Are you in love?"

"I don't know," said the coyote.

"How does your stomach feel?"

"Empty, and my heart aches. Yet I have had a good meal of venison."

"Your stomach aches, you mean," said the heron. "The

stomach is the seat of love, I have discovered."

"The doves speak of nothing but the heart and the soul," said the coyote.

"The doves, as the world knows, are fools," said the heron. "I will prove to you that the heart, emotionally speaking, is merely a poetic name for the stomach."

"I listen, madam," said the coyote, "with breathless interest."

"Go fasting for three days," said the heron. "If you find yourself in love on an empty stomach, then come back and talk to me about the heart. Otherwise, I don't wish to hear another word about it." She added: "Is she young?"

"She?" said the coyote. "Do you mean my mother?"

"I mean your lady, your beautiful one."

"There is no lady in the case," said the coyote.

The heron opened her great bill again in a fit of laughter so hearty that she spread her wings and shook all her graceful, drooping plumes.

"In love with love! Excuse me a moment . . . ," she interrupted herself hastily. "There is a clever young frog about to come out and sing for his lady. He's been popping his head up to the surface every moment, and I yearn to hear his voice."

With that, she drew back her head, and curved her neck until it almost disappeared against her shoulders and along her back. It looked like a harpoon mounted on a handful of flexible cable, with this difference, that a brain lived in the spearhead and the strands of the rope were exquisitely tapered muscle.

Weeds obscured the coyote's view of the frog, but a moment later its voice rose. Its very first quiver was cut off by the javelin stroke of the heron, which lifted its head with the frog kicking violently in its beak.

"Delicious . . . music," said the heron, and swallowed. She dropped back her head again and closed her eyes, murmuring: "Exquisite song. So young, and so poetic, too." Then, with a fanning stroke of her wings, she turned her attention to the coyote.

"You're a lover of music, I see," said the coyote, grinning sympathetically.

"But I love the musicians more than their song," she replied. "I've never had enough of them, really. But I go on day after day studying them . . . taking the subject into me, as you might say."

"And very well said, too," said the coyote. "But how about love?"

"Laughter makes a good digestion," said the heron, "but you'll have me frightening all of these tender little artists to death, in a short time. My dear boy, what shall I tell you about love?"

"Tell me what it is," he begged.

The heron continued her sardonic smile and fixed her glittering eye on him. Yet he knew that the same eye was viewing every item of the water and the reeds.

"Tell me what the sky is," said the heron.

"I don't know," said the coyote, "except that my mother said that it is the floor of heaven."

"A ridiculous definition," said the heron. "Or rather, not a definition at all. If we are to talk, let us be precise."

"I can't give you a clearer idea," said the golden coyote.

"I don't think you can," she said. "You can't tell how far away it is, either. It is as blue as water, but, though I have flown so high that the Kendal Mountains looked like a fog beneath me and the clouds were under my feet, yet I can assure you that I never came close enough to that water to drink. I hope you follow me?"

"Not quite so high," said the golden coyote.

The heron continued her smile. "You seem to have some wit," she said. "I mean to point out that the sky is a mystery, and so is love. There is a difference between them, however."

"And what is that?" he asked.

"The sky is pleasant, and love is damned unpleasant. Excuse me, but I can't help swearing when I think of it."

"Is it so disagreeable?"

"Worse," she told him, "than chills and fever. And very similar, in a way. You never know when the attack will return. I, who can stand in water while the ice is forming around my legs and yet never have known cold feet . . . I, who have killed two hawks in my time . . . even I, my dear youngster, grow cold to the pit of my stomach at the mention of love, and more frightened than by the stoop of an eagle. The clumsy brutes. I must say they are all thumbs in their flying."

"You laugh at it, however . . . love, I mean to say," said the coyote.

"Creatures of any spirit always should laugh at things that cannot be understood," she said. "It is always done in the best circles. You ask me about love, but I can only answer you with a few epigrams."

"I shall be glad to hear them," he said, "if they will tell me the truth about love."

"An epigram is to truth," she said, "as a duck pond to the ocean, for both contain the blue of heaven. And let me tell you, in the beginning, that love does much, but mice do everything."

"I don't understand," said the coyote.

"They fill the stomach," the heron replied. "You must try to think hard when I am speaking to you, because I hate to explain myself. Explanations always are shallow. Take this to heart . . . 'He who runs from love shall find it.' "

"Ah?" said the coyote, more bewildered than ever.

"Love," she went on, "is a secret that should be left in the nest. It is a disease that only one doctor can cure."

"I hope I'm allowed to ask the doctor's name?" he said.

"Time!" the heron snapped, with great satisfaction. "Love sits in the stomach and dines on the brain. Love has no mercy. Love laughs in the dark. Is your brain spinning?"

"It is, a little," said the coyote.

"I nearly always dazzle people," said the blue heron. "If not with my plumes, with my conversation. But now we have made so much noise with our talk that the musicians here are discouraged. I don't blame you. Lovers cannot help talking. In parting, let me tell you this a. . . ." She spread her feathers and, springing up, began to beat the air with hollow wings, her long legs trailing behind her, while her final speech drifted back and down to him: "A coyote in love is but half a coyote." She was almost out of his hearing when she added: "The last word is the wisest."

So she disappeared, flying low above the river, and the coyote, backing to dry land, went thoughtfully down the valley.

The day still lingered. The moon, rising behind the Kendal Woods, was rosy gold above and purple with mist across its lower face. At the sight of it, a song rose in the throat of the golden coyote that he never had sung before, and yet he had it by heart. It went up with a quick yipping, and then wailed and rang across the valley of the Musquash.

He paused to breathe. He was trembling with sorrow and delight. But before he could sing again and ease his heart with the new music, he heard a thin answer barked from the southern hills. Never had he heard a voice like this before. As though the strings of his soul were set and tense and tuned for it, the sound went through and through him. He turned toward it. The dusky grass was blurred by his speed as he fled for that sound, and, sweeping over a hilltop, he had to check himself with stiffly braced legs, for he had almost blundered into a group of three of his kind.

One was an old fellow who continually shrugged his shoulders at the itch; another was the biggest and heaviest coyote he ever had seen, a forty-five pounder if ever one stepped, a magnificent animal with a very dark coat and enough black at the tip of his tail to have pointed half a dozen ordinary prairie wolves. He was a true brush coyote, such as rarely appeared in the Kendal Mountains. But it was the third of the group that made the heart of the golden coyote leap. She came straight forward and almost touched his nose with hers. She was young. She was slender. She was soft and gray as a mouse.

"How beautiful!" gasped the golden coyote. "Your eyes are as bright as the moon in still water. How beautiful you are!"

"Stand back," said the brush coyote, bristling his mane.

The golden coyote shrank.

"What a bother!" exclaimed the gray beauty. "Are we to have nothing but fighting, and no conversation whatever?"

"I'm tired of talk," said the brush coyote. "You know what I am and what I can offer you. I don't intend to be fubbed off and fubbed off while you listen to the gibbering of a mangy old fool like that first fellow or the maunderings of this half-grown puppy."

"The loudest voice is not always the sharpest tooth," remarked the veteran coyote from the background.

"Then stand up to me and I'll prove it," said the big fellow. "I despise talk, as I said before, and I know perfectly well that this matter will have to be settled with a fight. It always is. And you know it, too," he added to the lady.

"I know that you are all three very brave and big and handsome and wise," she said. "And it's a beautiful evening, besides."

She smiled at the golden coyote, and his heart swelled. He could not take his glance from her.

"It is love," he found himself saying. "Oh, sweet, sweet love. Oh, pain."

"He's a fool," said the brush coyote. "Sweet and painful. It makes me tired to hear such rot. And you, my dear," he continued to her, "know perfectly that the coyote for you is the tried and proved provider. Now, I ask you to look at me, and then at that withered old scandal-monger, and lastly at this thing." He advanced with a proud, stiff step toward the young prairie wolf, and the latter shrank a little, though he at least had courage not to budge his feet.

"This," said the brush coyote, towering and mighty.

"You're very harsh," said the lady. "I think he talks extremely well."

"Stuff," he said. "Talk never killed ground dog."

"Talk might keep wives from poisoned baits, however," said the veteran in the background.

"I've a mind to break your back," said the brush coyote.

"Do," replied the other. "Do try to catch me."

"The coward would never stand for an instant," the big fellow pointed out. "He's another talker. What in the name of heaven can you offer to a wife?"

"Experience," said the other, "which is better than fat antelope. I don't pretend to the sharpest tooth, but my home never has lacked mice, at least. Luxury I don't pretend to offer . . . security I do. The best advice, mind you, is worth having. You, for instance, let two of your wives run into an early death, and your litters starved to death."

"I've a mind to finish you now!" growled the brush coyote. "Who can prevent bad fortune?"

The older coyote sat down and scratched his ear. "The bigger the leg, the snugger the trap fits," he said. "I hope you won't be lured by the beef and brawn of this big boaster, my child. Brains are what count in this world. As for his talk, what does it amount to? Let's be practical. He can't feed you puma or bear meat. And even if he could, would you want it? On the other hand, I don't want to boast, but simply to advise you of the truth. I have eaten eggs from the chicken house of man."

At that word, the gray lady almost dropped to her stomach, and showed her teeth, bright and sharp as icicles, and the clear pink of her gums fascinated the golden coyote.

"How beautiful you are," he said. "Oh, this is love, this is love."

"I have eaten chicken eggs myself, for that matter," said the brush coyote sharply. "What else have you to offer?"

"The taste of tender lamb is not unknown to me, either," said the oldster, "and veal, well hung. I am familiar with young pork . . . a delicious thing in autumn. I have killed rats in the very cellar of man's house. Now, my young braggart, how will you match this?"

"I have done everything that you have done," said the brush coyote, "and more besides. But you're not worth considering, except to sharpen a tooth on your carcass. I wish you would take a swim before you fight, if you have the heart for that."

"Well, well," said the other, "the biggest coyote is not always the soonest married . . . and the strength of the weak has caught many a field mouse. You have lived off man, you say?"

"I have," said the brush coyote. "I have looked through man's cave, at the opening that is closed with ice."

"You mean a window, I suspect?" yawned the veteran.

At this, the lady laughed, and the brush coyote grew furious.

"Talk, talk, talk," he said. "I'm tired of it. And here's a young idiot who has neither words nor deeds to offer. This! Is he a wolf, a dog, or a coyote? I'm sure he has features of them all, but I never saw a mongrel, if he is not one. What have you to offer, my young friend?"

The golden coyote hardly heard the insults. He could only stare at the yellow eyes of the lady, and now he sighed.

"How beautiful. How beautiful. Your muzzle is so exquisitely slender that you could eat the egg of a partridge and leave half the shell unbroken."

"A poet, by heaven," said the brush coyote, and laughed loudly.

"He seems a very mannerly young man," said the gray coyote. "You needn't bully him so."

"What can you do? What can you do? Are you going to stand there mooning about beauty all night?" asked the brush coyote.

The golden coyote roused himself. "I've heard a great deal of talk about the way you make a fool of man," he said, "but let me tell you the truth. I, the golden coyote, have gone down to the house of man, whose smoke we smell at the present moment, and I have stood in the doorway, and have taken food from the hand of man, and have carried it away, and eaten."

There was a pause, then a loud burst of derision.

He looked at the lady, and his heart ached to see that, although she had dropped her head, she, also, was laughing.

"Furthermore," said the golden coyote, "I shall go this moment and do it."

"Let him go," said the brush coyote, "I have heard bragging before, but this is interesting. He is probably a halfwit."

"He is only young," said the veteran. "By all means, let's go along and watch. My friend, don't let us keep you, if this is your time."

"Very well," said the golden coyote, and, wheeling, he fairly flew across the hills until he came to the sight of the house of man, with its great, bright, far-seeing eyes, and the shadowy forms of new-built barn and sheds, and the skeleton tangle of new fencing, as well. Then he fell back to a stalking trot. The three followed at his heels.

"I believe he means to do it," said the gray lady. "Is he in his right mind? Man . . . and guns . . . and poison . . . and death. Why I actually tremble to think of it."

"Save your trembling," said the veteran quietly. "He will find an excuse that will make him dodge long before he comes to that open doorway."

The golden coyote heard, and this was the challenge that drove him straight into the eye of the rising breeze, past the tidings of new-cut hay, of resinous, freshly worked pine boards, of pigs, and sheep, and sweet-breathing cattle, and horses, and the dire scent of hunting dogs, of oil and iron, at last, and the dreadful presence of man himself.

For the coyote stood now in the shaft of light that came through the open doorway. To the side, the dogs leaped to the length of their chains with a furious clamor, but he knew that iron held them, and he went straight on until his forepaws rested on the threshold.

Once before he had been there. Starvation, on that day, had driven him. Man himself rose from a table and shouted. The dogs were still at the voice of the master, as all the animals are still when the God of the coyotes thunders in heaven. The woman rose, also, and the little girl, crying: "The golden coyote! Look at him, Daddy! Don't stir! Look! He knows us, now. He's not afraid. Good dog . . . good boy. . . ."

"He has dog in him," said man, the hunter. "There never was a coyote with an eye like that. Now if we had sense, we'd shoot that thief before he gets back his tooth for uncooked chicken."

"Oh, Daddy," said the child. "Shoot the golden coyote that killed the elk for us? Where would we be?"

"I was talkin', only," man admitted, growling. "There, honey. You've had your hand on him before. Give him that chop, and try to get him inside. Look at him, will you, just as brave as a lion."

Brave? The golden coyote trembled. Fear stiffened his hair like frost, for their voices and their faces enchanted him with terror, and the odor of oil and iron, which is the odor of death-on-the-wing, was rank in his nostrils.

But he saw the girl coming. He feared her least of all, and he could remember the night of his puppyhood when her arm had held him like a collar, and her hand had kept off the teeth of the dogs. She came to him now, tiptoeing, speaking as gently as the doves that had complained of love, and there was food in her hand. It came closer. It was a span away.

Then the coyote's head darted, and, snatching the prize, he whirled into the outer darkness.

"He'll come again. We'll have him," said the voice of man.

He found the three waiting. At the feet of the gray lady he laid his prize.

"Poison," said the brush coyote jealously. "Don't touch it, my dear."

He was much too late.

"Delicious," she said. "And it carries the taste of fire. How wonderful you are!" she went on to the golden coyote. "When I actually saw you standing in the doorway, so big, so handsome, with the light glimmering on you, the light of man . . . I was so frightened that I nearly turned away and ran. But, of course, I stayed to watch. I never have seen such a thing or even heard of it before today. Such courage never was shown before by a coyote."

"Coyote? Rot!" said the brush coyote, writhing in jealous anger. He stalked up to the other and planted himself squarely between his rival and the gray beauty. "Even the birds in the trees are chatting about it," he said. "The blue jays are laughing about the cross-bred mongrel that calls himself a coyote. You son of a yellow dog!"

The golden coyote felt his brain burst into flame. He would as soon have faced a timber wolf as this big warrior, but that temporary madness thrust him straight forward. The wind of his leap was whistling in his teeth as he dove directly for the throat of the brush coyote.

That seasoned campaigner was much taken by surprise. He had fought fifty times before, but always there had been much cursing, snarling, boasting before the final battle began, with skirmishing. This headlong charge like the rush of a ferret was not the tactics of a coyote, yet the brush coyote side-leaped in plenty of time, if only he had been on firm ground. But it was not firm, it was a treacherous, sandy surface, at this point; one hind paw slipped, and the long fighting jaw of the golden coyote closed on his throat. Now, in coyote style, he should have ripped and torn, then sprung back again. But he did not. He knew very well the lunges, the parries, the time thrusts, and the saber strokes of coyote battle. He had practiced them himself since his puppyhood, but in this blind fury another instinct overmastered him, and with closed eyes he held his grip, deeper and deeper.

A weight dragged down on the jaw of the golden coyote. He relaxed his hold and, stepping back, stared at the limp body of the enemy. The red tongue lolled; the open eyes were no brighter than muddy water.

The golden coyote began to shake. "It is death. It is death," he said. "I have killed him for your sake." He turned.

She was not there. All the valley lay naked before him, with the smiling moon at its farther end. He thought of the mangy old coyote, and how he had sat down to scratch. Sickness and weakness poured through him, for he had faced death twice for her sake.

He was so weary, now, that he did not even jog, but walked slowly back over the slopes. The wind still rose. On his own hillside he pointed his nose up it and breathed the scent of the budding trees, saw the Musquash flashing in the bottom of the dark valley like a streak of sunlight on the bottom of a pool, and out of the northeast heard again the droning horn that sounded in the upper cañon. It appeared to him that the world was too big, that he had shrunk to the size of a week-old puppy.

"Mother!" he called, but, getting no answer from the cave above him, he dragged himself up the slope toward it. She was angry, of course, because he had run off, and, therefore, she would not speak.

"Mother!" he whimpered again, coming up to the little shoulder before the cave.

But there was neither scent nor sound of her. And from the shadow beside the cave a form stepped out into the full brightness of the moon that turned it all to silver, except the dark tail tip and the yellow eyes.

A greater tremor of weakness came over the golden coyote. "Ah, is it you?" he said.

"Darling!" she answered.

IV

The golden coyote grinned as though he were scratching himself. He was very tired. Since moonrise he had helped carry the five little ones from the old hillside to this, where the forest stretched around them like the horns of an elk, and then he had caught mice and brought them three at a time, winding up with a rabbit that had run him gaunt. The moon was now a thin shred of silk above the sunrise, and he felt all as faint and worn himself.

"White Foot, Light Foot, Shiver-Nose, Tingle-Toes," she crooned in the cave.

"If that's a poem," he said, "I know it by heart already. And if it's a song, I wish you would finish it."

"The children like it," she said.

"No doubt they do," he said.

"Poor little darlings," she murmured absently.

They were to be pitied, he judged, because they had such a father. The injustice of such a remark rankled in him, but he could not think of an appropriate answer. He wanted to sleep, but his very ears twitched with impatience. He knew that it was rash to rouse her temper and her tongue, but the imp of the perverse urged him on.

"White Foot, Light Foot, Tingle-Nose, Shiver-Toes," he mocked.

"You have it wrong," she snapped. "If you can't remember the simplest poetry. . . ."

"Poetry?" he scoffed. *"Ah-h-h!"* His yawn was followed by a moment of deadly silence.

She then remarked politely: "You've heard better, no doubt?"

Shall I, or shall I not? he asked of his irritable heart. Then: "I have listened to the doves at sunset," he replied.

She did not speak, but he heard her shake herself and knew that she had stood up. With a half-pleasant sense of trouble coming, he looked to the south, where a thin arm of smoke was standing above the woods and putting a ghostly hand flat against the sky.

"You've been eating grass again and you've upset your digestion," she decided.

"Have I?" he said. He hated to be explained.

"As a matter of fact," she said, "when I notice some of your habits, I can't help remembering what the brush coyote said . . . that your father must have been at least half dog."

"I thought the brush coyote's talk was as dead as himself," said the golden coyote.

"There, there," she soothed him. "You see that I've given you a chance to put your best foot forward again."

"Ah, yes," he said. "Females always give one chances for war and for work."

"Work," she said. "Work!"

The young ones began to make little blind noises of complaint and yelps of chilly loneliness, so that he guessed she was coming out to him. He did not turn his head, though a faint tremor passed twitching through the loose hide along his back.

"Work," she repeated from the very mouth of the cave. "A great deal you know about it!"

"If I haven't the profile of a greyhound . . . may they all go blind and lame with a curse . . . from hunting all day and house-moving all night, then I haven't looked at myself in a pool. I have no more stomach than a puma in February," he retorted.

"There's nothing more unhealthy than fat," she answered, "and a lean belly makes a sharp tooth. Besides, no one can trust the images in a pool . . . they're so distorted with ripples, and what not."

"I'm talking about facts, not pictures," he said. "I feel the bones of my chest every time I lie down . . . working all day," he repeated, "and house-moving all night."

"You know as well as I do," said the helpmate, "that I found the track of man within fifty yards of our front door."

"Men have hardly any eyes, and no nose whatever," he answered.

" 'What a beautiful evening,' said the grouse, as the horned owl swooped on it," she murmured mockingly. "Well, no one can teach wisdom to a lazy coyote."

"Lazy?" he said, his gorge rising again.

"You know perfectly well," she replied tersely, "that even if there wasn't the slightest danger in the old home, the little ones need a change of air." She went on, in a changed tone: "It's so delicious here. Do you smell the fat little ground squirrels in the low ground? But what's that scent of wood smoke in the air?"

"You can see for yourself," he answered.

"Is it coming this way?"

"How can I tell? Fire is the only other thing that has a mind that can't be read and that changes with the wind."

She pretended not to understand, but harped on the subject that she had just been avoiding.

"As for work, I don't know what you're talking about. What am I doing all day long, and all night? Feeding, and washing . . . washing and feeding. No end. No stop. And no gratitude, either. And all you have to do is to walk through the beautiful forest, eating three mice for every one you bring home to me, where I lie in the damp darkness, working, working, working, never complaining, giving myself for the sake of five beautiful young lives. . . ."

"Oh, rot," said the golden coyote. "They look like five foolish rabbits to me . . . all foot and no head. They'll be half-wits, if they ever grow up to be called aright. . . ."

He jumped as he spoke, but he jumped a little too late. The keen teeth of his mate nipped him in the flank, not once, but three times. She even ran a little beside him, still biting, and whining in utter fury. "Cannibal! Cannibal!" she cried.

The golden coyote almost ran his hind legs up to the front ones, he worked so hard, but, when he got to a safe distance, he turned and gasped: "You can't take a joke, my dear. Of course, I didn't mean it."

She paced up and down before the cave, still frantic. "Cannibal, cannibal!" she howled. "Oh, yellow dog!"

This insult made him tip up on his hind legs, and he yipped with fury. "I'm going away!" he cried.

"I hope you do! I hope you do!"

"Do you? You ingrate . . . you . . . you . . . I'll never come back, either!"

"I don't want you. I hope you don't. You half-breed! You son of a three-legged beggar and a yellow dog . . . dog . . . dog!" She screamed the last.

The golden coyote was sick with rage. He wanted to rush back and thrash her into a gentler vocabulary, but he knew that not even a mountain lion cares to trouble a mother and her young. What increased his fury to the bursting point was that he could not think of a single strong response but had to keep hopping about in his ecstasy. At last he whirled and shot away over smooth and rough through the forest, at such a rate and so blindly that he almost ran into man and man's daughter, as the two walked happily through the cool of the morning woods. All in a flash there rushed upon him the odor of oil and steel, and powder, and of man himself, and then, as he swerved, he had a sight of them, and he heard the shrill voice of the little girl crying: "Look, look! It's the golden coyote again! Look!"

He tried to dissolve himself with utter speed and turn into a yellow-copper streak, but, as he looked back, he saw that man was not pointing the rifle.

He almost forgot his anger, in the overmastering greatness of his fear, but then, as he reached secure distance, he slowed to a stealthy walk—he never was quite at home in the sun-splashed gloom of the woods—and began to blame all of his recent alarm on his wife. She was, he felt, the mere beginning and starting point of misfortune.

He heard running water before him and started for it to take a needed drink—fear dries the throat like the loss of blood—when the odor of the king of the forest crossed him. It made his hair bristle along his back; it numbed his brain, for the scent was rank with nearness. Then he forced himself to remember that all the brains of a grizzly cannot quite equal the fleet foot of a coyote.

He heard a splashing sound, and the noise of a wet fall, followed by flopping. Fish? He dropped to his belly and went forward like a cat to explore. So he came through a thicket and saw a little stream, on the edge of which a big stone jutted, and on the stone lay the king himself—seven hundred pounds of loosely robed wisdom and might. His ambidextrous forepaws drooped over the side of the rock, and, even as the golden coyote arrived, his majesty flicked a good-size fish out of the water. It sailed back like a ray of silver light and landed solidly on the ready fangs of the thief. Five more fat fellows already lay on the bank, and the coyote was wishing the king good hunting with all his heart—the tail of the last fish, in fact, was just going down his throat—when something made the bruin turn.

He did not seem angry. He merely smiled at the coyote, and, coming to the five fish, he disposed of each as a single mouthful.

"Your majesty," said the golden coyote, choking a little on the first few words, "your majesty is in perfect health, we trust?"

"We?" said the grizzly, and lifted his head, and moved his pig nose to read the air beyond the other.

"All of your subjects," said the golden coyote, "speak for one another . . . all of your faithful subjects . . . I say nothing of the gray wolf, the slandering thief . . . or of the bobcat, or the lion on Mount Hope. I hope you will discipline that loud-mouthed boaster, someday."

The king itched a ponderous shoulder against a spruce, and the tree trembled from its roots. "I'm not interested in fighting," he said. "It spoils the teeth and ruins the claws." He raised a forepaw and looked down at it with judicious eyes. "In short, I am a philosopher, my son, and I never trouble my head about loud talk or, here and there, a lost fish."

The point of this remark was not lost on the golden coyote, but he pretended to take it seriously. "I have followed you before," he said, "and always have admired your liberality. Many a rabbit has run from you into my teeth, and many a mouse has slipped from your paw under mine. In fact, the waste from your table is a banquet on mine, your majesty. That is why I have spent so much time in your company, although I never before felt like pressing myself forward too much."

The bear wrinkled his nose again. "Yes," he said, "I think you're the one that one day scared a fat young deer within reach of my paw."

The coyote half closed his eyes and sighed. "My duty and my pleasure," he said, his mouth watering enviously at the memory, "and I still remember the sound of his ribs, crunching under your stroke."

"No wasted effort, no wasted effort," grunted the bear, who was not above being touched by flattery, it appeared. "The blow that kills the game should carve it, also. You are married, I see."

"You see?" exclaimed the golden coyote, looking apprehensively over his shoulder. When he glanced back again, he found on the face of the bear a wider and redder smile than ever.

"I can tell," said the bruin, "by a vacant look in your eye, which some people call the second thought, and also by the line of your stomach, and the wretched state of your coat. A glossy coat means a single mind." Then he added: "I may say that is original."

"How profound you are," said the coyote. "May I ask if you believe in matrimony?"

"If you wish for an answer," said the grizzly, "come along with me. I think best at table, and, therefore, I always like to eat when I talk. Though the conversation, as you may guess, is my first aim."

"I haven't a doubt," said the golden coyote, and, looking at the large barrel of the king, he added politely: "I imagine that you could keep talking for a very long time."

The bear was now leading the way and the coyote followed at a respectful distance.

"Long thoughts are the best thoughts," said the bear.

He flicked out a great forepaw, and with it smothered in the grass the squeak of a mouse. That morsel he transferred dexterously to his great red tongue and continued: "But little words fill in the corners, as you may say."

The golden coyote licked his chops and said nothing.

They came out into a meadow where a great ant heap stood in the center like the small swarming capital of a fertile plain.

The grizzly woofed with pleasure. "Sit down, sit down," he grunted, "for there is nothing like eating at one's ease."

He set the example by taking his place beside the ant hill. First he sniffed it, then he knocked off the top dexterously and laid his paw beside it. Out bubbled the big ants; the sight of them set the golden coyote itching up to his very eyelids, but when the paw of the bear had been thickly covered, he raised it and licked it clean on both sides, then gave a touch or two of his tongue to his forearm, where some of the most rapid brigades of the ants were clambered.

"Don't they bite holes in your tongue?" gasped the coyote.

The king simply overlooked this question, as though it were too childish to deserve an answer.

"A little acid," he said, "will always stimulate the stomach." Then he laid his paw on the nest, to have it instantly blackened with a fresh myriad. "But as for marriage, I should say that a deaf husband and a blind wife make the only happy couple, and the married bear is seven years older the first day."

"Then you're not married?" asked the coyote with interest equally divided between watching this acrid diet and his own home problem.

"Married?" said the bear, licking the second supply thoughtfully from his wet paw. "That depends on the way you look at it. If you mean living in the same house, no, I am not. If you mean keeping the same wife from year to year . . . no again. But to go more deeply into the matter"—here he opened the ant nest to its roots with delicate precision—"I do believe that one owes to the world a physical duty. Thought is not all that should be preserved of one."

He lowered his head, and the coyote saw with a shudder of the stomach that the king was eating little white things together with the brave ants that flocked to defend them. From the depths of the ground, as it were, the voice of the king continued: "But I find the chief difficulty is the lack of conversation. They can't discuss. They must be taught. And yet the first step toward wisdom is to learn never to lecture wife nor cub . . . puppy, I believe you call your young?"

"Yes," said the coyote.

The bear rose. "So ends that point," he said with a sigh, looking down at the ravished nest. "But let us go on. The world is filled with good ideas, if one will only hunt for them with a careful nose, and, upon my soul. . . . No, is it possible? It is! It is! Yes, it is true!" He sat up fully, wabbling his nose almost like a rabbit, and his mouth drooled with expectant pleasure. "Almost directly up the wind," said the grizzly, and started forward with such rapidity that the golden coyote had to gallop to keep up.

"What is it?" he asked. "A nest of mice?"

"Bees," said the bear.

"Good heavens," said the coyote. "They'll sting your eyes out . . . they'll sting. . . ."

"Stings for relish, honey for sweet. Bees, bees! Wise little workers! Delicious thought!" said the bruin.

He splashed through a little creek. Beyond it he came to a great old tree, half of whose branches were dead. The singing of bees reached the coyote and made him flatten his ears. That, and the deep rumble of workers inside the cave, myriads of wings.

The grizzly stood up with dripping mouth. "No climbing to do," he said. "Not a whit, but all in easy reach. Now, we were speaking of marriage . . . my status." Here he inserted the claws of both forepaws inside a comparatively small hole. "For my part, I believe that beauty, the rainbow, and the echo soon pass. I am, in one word, a worshiper of the practical."

As he spoke, with the might of his great forearms, with the chisel edges of his claws, he ripped the half-rotten outer shell of the trunk away. There was an explosion, a roar of wings, an upward burst of shining smoke that surrounded the head of the bear, and then showered down over head, and neck, and shoulders, a thick powdering of golden dust.

The king had buried his muzzle in masses of waxy comb whose bursting cells gave out a torrent of honey. The coyote shrank in terror to the ground as he heard the death-drumming of the furious bees, but his mouth watered as the perfume floated out in an expanding cloud and drenched the place.

Clotted and indistinct, the voice of the bear issued from the midst of the treasure: "Not that I despise beauty, pure and ethereal as snow flowers, white-tipped buckwheat, the monkshood, the pink, the purple aster, daisies, buttercups, trembling harebells, and the forget-me-not . . . ah, the forget-me-not! All the cool-breathing spring in delicate fragrance. Not that I despise love, rich as the summer of the yellow pond lily, the wealth of the black-eyed Susans, columbine and larkspur, lupine and yarrow . . . gathered and golden . . . warm summer . . . golden love . . . delicious. . . ."

From the crushed comb masses an amber stream dripped over the lip of the opening and ran slowly down the outer bark.

The grizzly tore the hole still wider and disappeared to the shoulders. "But speaking profoundly," he said dimly, from the depths of the tree—from the very ground, as it were—"speaking profoundly, love is a sweet moment, which for the instant seems rich and maturely ripened to the very bottom hive, but which"—here he backed away from the tree and banished the robbed bees with a wave of his royal paw—"but which is soon ended, soon ended . . . and then away, my young friend, and put love behind us. . . ."

He advanced into the stream and drank liberally, then clambered the farther bank with a sound of water and honey swishing and rumbling in his great belly.

"For who," said the grizzly, "would fail to realize that half the beauty of love is its strangeness, and familiarity does nothing but show us the callus on the nose, and the broken foreclaw, and other defects . . . other defects. Leave love for the spring, and be a philosopher the rest of the year, with a long sleep to round off the seasons."

"Oh, most kingly of bears and wisest of kings," said the golden coyote, "tell me which way the fire is coming."

"Fire?" said the grizzly, shutting his eyes and standing erect to the full of his height. "Is there a fire? Yes, yes, upon my word, there is a fire in the south."

"Of course there is," said the coyote rather impatiently, for now a great dark column was rising, and the scent on the southern wind was both of smoke and of heat. "But will it come this way?"

The grizzly dropped down on all fours and shook his head. "Fire is a matter that I never look into," he said. "It is the one mind which I never wish to fathom. It may give me roast venison tomorrow, and a dead range for a month afterward. I have known such things to happen."

"Who could have started that fire?" asked the coyote. "What man . . . ?"

"Man? Stuff!" said the grizzly. "Man has nothing to do with it. It is true that he is fool enough to play with it, trying to show that he is not afraid of it . . . but, as a matter of fact, fire lives all the year underground."

"Good heavens," said the coyote, lifting his forepaws quickly, in turn. "Underground?"

"Dining on deep roots, quietly eating the lower, moist masses of the pine needles and the forest humus. There it lives, sleeping, breathing gently, until it is tired of resting, and then the giant stirs. Sometimes he thrusts up only one red hand. Sometimes he stands up and puts his head into the sky. And at that time . . . well, well! . . . I never look in his face."

The little exclamation that interrupted his last sentence came as he turned over a dead log and saw its moist underside littered with grubs, white and fat. He began to eat them leisurely.

"Can you devour those?" asked the coyote, between amazement and disgust. "Can you eat everything?"

"Like the fire . . . yes," said the grizzly. "My cousin, the fire. . . ."

"Is he your cousin?"

"He is the only thing in the world as strong as I am," answered the grizzly contentedly, "and, therefore, of course, he must be a member of my family."

"One thing at least is sure," said the golden coyote. "I am going to lead an independent life."

"You mean one without a wife?" The bear looked up as he spoke and wriggled his nose, which with him was the usual sign of reflection.

"I mean that," said the golden coyote. "No more hunting for seven stomachs. One will do."

"Now, that is all very well," answered the grizzly, dropping his head toward the grubs again. "But, after all, there is nothing that has such a sharp tooth as remorse. Don't let it get a throat hold."

This feast of grubs, newly exposed, attracted a number of wasps, and, when he saw them, the grizzly backed away, with a grunt.

"What do you mean by the sharp tooth of remorse?" asked the coyote.

"Well," said the bear, "many that are brave by day are lonely by night, and you can work out that for yourself, or else ask the wasps, if you understand their language. For my part, I never hear them buzz without wanting to sneeze."

He started off at once, and in his great bad humor he strode through a thicket of berry bushes whose thorns made the golden coyote recoil. He was about to take a longer way around to rejoin this wise companion, but, as he turned, the south wind struck him fairly in the face, and he saw above the heads of the trees an uprushing of smoke, colored gray-green. It rose as if from a hundred funnels, with a forced draft behind it, and it presented a wide front. The coyote could see no flame, but now and then there was an upbursting of sparks, and the wind was heavy with the smell of the smoke.

What the bear had last said stuck in the mind of the coyote more than all of the wisdom about a solitary life that had preceded it. He thought of the cold, dark night, and the lonely gleam of the stars overhead, and an empty cave for company. At this moment, he recalled the five little ones not as gaping maws, but as ridiculous little clowns that one day would be wise coyotes. He thought of his wife, also, divorced from her temper as a mother, and as he first had seen her, young, slender, and soft and gray as a mouse.

With this, he struck a good pace down the valley.

As he went, it seemed to him that all of the life in the lower valley was streaming up toward him, blown by the still rising wind. Above him a blue jay flashed like a bright jewel, flying very low, rising and dipping over the tops of the trees. A magpie flitted past, and then came a doe, followed by two young ones.

One of them surely should have made food for him, on another day, but now he was occupied by another thing. He regarded their fear more than their fat sides.

And he heard the mother panting in a voice meant only for her own ears: "Oh, where shall we go? Oh, where shall we go?"

Actually she turned around the next stump and with her exhausted young ones bolted straight back toward the fire.

"Fools have a short life," gasped the golden coyote to himself, and fled onward with a redoubled pace.

When he broke from the last screen of the forest, his heart swelled with gratitude to see before him the obscure entrance of the cave on the side of the little hill, but once again it seemed to him, as on the night before, that his wife had chosen foolishly, because the forest trees were so near. And those bearers of fire were to his eyes now twice as lofty and as dense as ever before.

He came to the entrance of the cave with a rush, and almost got the teeth of his wife in his throat, as a result. She jumped back, stiff-legged, when she realized that this was no stranger.

"Why are you here?" asked the golden coyote. "The fire is coming as if it ran on legs, and straight for us."

"We are in our home," she replied, and added, panting: "Thank the God of the coyotes that you have come at last!"

"No thanks to your conduct, though," he reproved her.

"Oh," she said, "you always will be jumping at me in my nervous moment."

"How can I tell when that will come?" he demanded.

"If you had five children!" she whimpered.

"I have six," answered the golden coyote. "Now, get them out of the den while I think what we are to do."

He went to the door of the cave again, while his wife rapidly hustled the little ones out. The change in the scene was amazing. The fire, galloping like a horse, was charging toward them on an ever-widening front, and now he could see the red glow of the flames, cast upward on the thick sheeting of the smoke above them, That smoke blew in dense sheets, covering the sun's face, so that it shrank to a small thing, no bigger or brighter than a red harvest moon. Through that canopy of smoke the light fell with a brown stain upon trees and rocks that turned to sepia. The green of the upward-jutting fountains of the smoke was stronger than ever. The ghosts of trees seemed to be rising with it, wavering and trembling. But now and again the fires broke loose as they struck some tree covered with a more inflammable foliage, and then a pyramiding leap of red gold followed, high into the dusky heavens.

"What will become of us!" whined the mother.

"Trust to me," the golden coyote answered, though he was as appalled as she. "We must cross the valley and get back to the old cave. Take one, and I shall take another. Back through the hole in the wall."

It was a narrow cleft in the wall of the ravine just opposite to their cave, and though it was no wider than six feet at the top, fifty feet lower it still afforded a fairly clear passage through the barrier.

"Take Shiver-Nose," said the father. "You're never done talking about his wit and wisdom."

"Tush," she said. "He is the strongest, leave him for the last."

The golden coyote was amazed, but he did not argue. The way of a female had been beyond his understanding before this, but never more than now. So he picked up the little one that lovingly she touched with her nose, while she said: "Gently, gently. Use the pressure of your tongue, too, and don't trot hard. All will be well. Courage, my darlings. We'll soon come back."

They left the mouth of the cave with the wailing of the deserted three shrill and high behind them. Overhead, the birds flew in a straight line, obviously bound away from trouble.

"Oh, for wings!" gasped the mother.

They fled across the valley. It was now a green forest through which they passed. The flying cloud masses of low-driven smoke so deeply tinged the sun's light that the very trees were brown.

They reached the gap. They passed through it, and found the

air strangely sweet, here, with a little cross-current drawn into their faces. They sped across the level. They reached the familiar hill, and how delightful was the well-trodden entrance of the old cave!

They went back. Behind them, the heavens were blue. Beyond the other ridge, it seemed as though giants were crushing earth and rocks to dry dust and flinging it into the zenith. But when they crossed the ridge again, it was almost impossible to realize the change.

All was brown fumes. The water in the runlets steamed. Breathing grew hard. One step cost the labor of ten. And through the deadly mist the golden coyote heard the frightened voices of young deer, and the mother crying: "What shall we do? What shall we do?"

He had to find his way by sense of direction rather than by the use of his half-blinded eyes. Scent was gone even from his mate, far keener of scent than he. So they came through inferno to the new cave.

"Take Shiver-Nose," he said.

"He is the strongest," she wheezed. "Save the weaker ones first."

And again they departed and left Shiver-Nose by himself.

The golden coyote could remember that he did not cry out, but stood silently at the door of the cave wagging his tail, a thing which no true-blooded coyote could be expected to do. So they journeyed the second time through the furious heat and the lung-eating smoke, and came to the blessing of the little gap in the cañon wall, and so on to their old home.

Four little coyotes now stood together, shivering, wailing, as though they were afraid of their deliverance, and the mother stood over them, licking them frantically, her eyes going here and there.

"Stay here," coughed the golden coyote, "and I'll go back alone."

"Oh, my brave . . . ," she said. "Go back. I shall go, also, as soon as I have taken breath for an instant."

He waited for no more, but dashed off. Duty led him. He was more afraid of it than of the fire. He had thought, when he started back, that nothing could be worse than the last visit, but this was all new, for the whole inner valley boiled with smoke, and, as he came out of the cut, he stopped, and flattened himself against the ground. The fire had struck a great tangle of trees, barren and dead since burning, long ago, and now, uprooted by the storms of the last fifty years and flung crosswise, an ideal heap of tinder with occasional lodgepoles standing tall and straight among the ruins.

The wall of fire struck this with a distinctly new voice, like a roar of many guns, or the thunder of a hurricane through a mountain pass. The flame rolled out like burning oil across the fallen trunks; when it struck the lodgepole pines, the enormous heat turned them incandescent. The golden coyote could see, through this terrible gloom, little purple balls of fire running up the trunks like frightened squirrels, and then the whole tree exploded into shooting flames and spark showers that dazzled his eyes more than the naked sun in the desert. This place of fallen trees became an inexhaustible torch that threw up mountains and perishing monuments of flame. The heat singed his coat. The smoke, bursting outward as from an explosion of gunpowder, curled along the ground. All around him the air was too black and thick for breathing, yet still he breathed, and still the fire shone terribly through this dense screen.

He reached a run of water and stood in it up to the nose, gasping. There was one more short burst to reach the new cave.

He leaped from the water, and lightened his coat with one shake, but, as he started onward for the cave, he saw man and the child of man close before him. Man stood no longer upright, but crawled upon all fours, with one leg trailing behind him and the foot turned awkwardly inward, so that even the golden coyote knew that the bone was broken. Now he lurched flat on the ground. Now he raised himself on trembling arms and waved the child ahead. She even went a running step or two, but returned at once, and threw up her arms in a gesture that made the heart of the coyote leap.

In the stress of the fire, he had pitied the deer, though they were food; now he pitied man, though he was fear itself, and he felt, moreover, an impulsion toward service such as no purebred coyote ever could have known.

He stood for a choking instant with a foreleg raised and his nose pointed toward the cave, which was in such easy reach. Then he ran straight to the fallen man and barked in his face.

"Look!" screamed the child. "The golden coyote!"

Man raised his fallen head. "He's luck," he said.

The coyote retreated, still barking, and choking, and barking again. And the man followed, though this new course was at right angles to the one he had been taking.

Then water dammed by falling trees burst onto the molten rocks in the fire pit and exploded again and again, until the ground shook beneath the golden coyote, and he saw in the black firmament clouds of sparks, like star streams.

The air grew more dense with smoke. To breathe was only to choke, yet, somehow, he kept life in, and, running back toward man, he barked again in his very face. And man followed him like a light through that darkness.

Firebrands from the explosion fell on the base of Mount Goodwin's slope. Five thousand feet long were those slopes, bearded with ancient forest, wrinkled with great ravines, tree-choked, also. In five seconds the fire front strode to the crest and there, uniting pressure of flames from all sides, cast high up into the rioting sky treetops.

The coat of the golden coyote smoked. His eyes bleared. But the pressure of forgotten centuries kept him with man until they entered the safe gate. The sweetness of the pure air, entering here in a gale like a draft to a fire, set him choking more than ever, but suddenly he could breathe and he remembered that man, also, was no longer helpless but once again was fear incarnate to all the world of beasts.

The golden coyote looked back. Through the end of the gap as through a window he saw the face of the fire front pass down the valley and over the hill where the new cave was burrowed.

Then he went home.

As he came near, he heard four small voices complaining, which made him cold with alarm, but when he rushed up the slope, he saw his wife lying at the entrance.

She was black with fire and with soot. One half of her head was blistered to the skin, and the opposite eye was closed so that she looked like a cartoon of her beautiful self, but to the golden coyote she looked as terrible and as imposing as some great statue of the God of the coyotes. For he knew she had gone to the new cave a third time.

She held herself stiffly, with her head high and her regard upon the distance, and across her forepaws lay Shiver-Nose, limp and dead.

V

Noise, for the golden coyote, never benumbed the brain or drowned all the senses, for the book of Nature in which he read was printed in capitals or small type for the nose. Therefore, he lay among the rocks by Poplar Creek while the earth trembled with the strength of the current rushing down in space and the waves of sound kept the delicate leaves of the trees quivering and turning bright and dark like a sunset breeze. He pointed his nose upward and studied the air with half-closed eyes of intense concentration and of hope, for this tumult of the creek was a voice calling to all the curious ears in the wilderness. The other waters ran placidly, with the autumn forest pouring gold and crimson and purple into them; the fallen leaves cruised calmly on, like little boats. But Poplar Creek had been suddenly recruited from the northern hills and now it ran madly down to join the Musquash, shouting, leaping, throwing up white arms.

This oddity delighted the coyote, but, being a father, a husband, and a son, with five stomachs to think of instead of one, there was no interest in the world to override his preoccupation with the next meal, and that was why he came to the edge of Poplar Creek. The perusal of the air told him that the king of the Musquash, the big grizzly himself, had come down to look over the stream and its noise, digging up and eating some grubs while he watched. Then he had fled suddenly for his delicate ears must have been overcome. The mountain lion, also, had lain out on some high branch, for the scent he cast was high along the air. But other things stirred nearer to the tooth of the golden coyote, and every moment he was reading tender items of mouse and rabbit and beautiful young deer.

It was a strange morning. Even the coming of the great forest fire had not been so weird and awful as the lights that now played mysteriously on the North Kendal Mountains. It was well before sunrise, otherwise he would have sworn that this was all some freak of golden sunshine, for sometimes yellow streams fell like water down the slopes, or huge balls rolled like flaming tumbleweed across the heights. Again he might have called it lightning, for the quiver and the spring of lightning were in its movements, but the great bright orders of the stars marched continually westward without passing through the stain of a single cloud. Only the approaching dawn made the eastern ranks dim.

This double mystery of the flooding creek and the mountain lights was enough to make the coyote expectant, and the howl of a timber wolf blown off the nearer hills exactly rounded the picture. It was a hunting cry that said as clearly as any word: "Venison!" Poetic joy filled the very soul of the golden coyote and made him rise a little among the rocks. He squatted again, at once. Through a cleft in the rocks he saw a black-tailed buck running from the valley for the hills, with a big timber wolf behind. He knew that lop-eared ruffian very well, the pattern of his waistcoat, the light in his eyes, the wicked red lolling of his tongue, and his speech that was all of blood and bones. Since the mule deer was not running in his direction, the coyote heartily wished that it might escape, but there seemed only the smallest chance of this, for though lop-ear was notoriously slow of foot, yet the blacktail must have been at the point of utter exhaustion, for its bounds were short and the wolf gained at every stride. He was on the verge of striking distance when he gained the rough ground. There at once the chase altered. The blacktail smote the ridges with all fours and soared from point to point, living in air, merely touching the earth, while the timber wolf dipped laboriously up and down through the hollows. So that bounding deer, like a miraculous ship sailing only on the crests of the waves, drew easily away, and lop-ear stopped his foolish chase.

That hunt was not ended, however. The deer had gained the crest of the first ridge and now ran in the very heart of the rosy sky, a flying black silhouette, when another wolf's cry rang dolefully from the height and the stag swerved into the first ravine. It was lop-ear's mate. The golden coyote knew her shrill voice instantly, and licked his lips with envious excitement as he saw lop-ear cut across to take up the hunt again. Ten seconds of breathing had restored him for the chase, and now he shot down the ravine at the heels of the mule deer. They came full on at the coyote, and he was so interested in the stagger in the buck's stride that he forgot to wonder at the poor deer's direction, for it was straight at Poplar Creek with its white torrent and all its gullet lined with sharp teeth. Yet the blacktail came on.

The coyote could see the foam that choked it, now, and the gloss of its large eyes, then it straightened for the riverbank. Lop-ear, realizing that even though the leap failed, it would mean a meal for the cold stomach of the creek rather than for himself, sprang at the hocks and missed by an inch. The mule deer reached the bank, smote it, and floated upward with trailing legs as though taking effortless flight. It was a mighty jump. Just clear of the threatening rocks it landed, sprawling. Lop-ear also leaped, but he went straight up into the air with a howl as though the unseen tooth of the rifle of man had bitten through him from flank to flank. The coyote heard that yell in the background of his mind, for his interest was in nearer work.

Just as the buck gathered himself for the next leap, when the legs were bunched and the muscles taut, the golden coyote sprang in and with all the weight of his body and the force of his wrenching neck he struck the hamstring of a rear leg. It parted with a shudder and a snap beneath his fang, and the deer fell struggling upon its side, straining up its head as it fought to recover footing.

As well have bent up its chin for the huntsman's knife. The coyote, running forward, flashed his sharp teeth across that tender throat, then leaped backward from the deadly sway of the horns, and stood there, licking his lips and regretting the fatal gush of red that followed, for he loved to be economical in his butchering. It was a big kill, a glorious day for him, and he smiled into the agonized eyes of the stag.

He could hear a softly moaning voice that was barely audible through the uproar of the stream: "Oh, God of the bounding deer, you gave me wings for the mountains, but I have come into the lowlands and, therefore, I am dying. You have given me the keenest of all ears to listen to the flesh-eaters . . . you have taught me the story of their foul scents in the air . . . you have sent the blue jay and others to warn me . . . but still I die by the tooth. I confess my sins. I looked from the bare uplands and coveted the sweet, thick grasses in the valley. I came down to the valley, and I am dead in it."

"You die, however, in a good cause," said the golden coyote dryly. "That is to say, five causes, if you prefer exactness."

"Brother," said the dying deer, "I forgive you."

"Let me console you," said the golden coyote. "I have been at a good many deathbeds, and, although I detest self-praise, I must admit that I have received some notice for my consolings. If you will listen to me, let me suggest that death comes to all things except to the God who maintains in the blue of the sky pleasant meadows filled with mice, and hen yards and sheep closes for good coyotes, with a deer spotted here and there just to give range and piquancy to our diet. Speaking of death, it was once said by a celebrated singer . . . a relative of mine, I believe . . . that the evil we do lives after us . . . but be assured you will be appreciated after death."

"Ah," said the deer, "you scorn and deride me now, but remember that we conquer today, but darkness waits for us tomorrow. Yet still I forgive you, for all the proud and the victorious are cruel."

"I am really sorry," said the coyote, licking his lips, "to see you bleed so much, and though I know that victory gives no account of her actions, and that he who wins it is always right, yet I wish to remind you that he who forgives gains the triumph."

"Do with me as you will," said the blacktail faintly. "My concern is with eternity. For my sinful way took me out of the bright mountains into the dusky valley. Then the deer God made me to hear in the midst of danger the singing and the shouting of water as if it were in my native mountains. I came to it and I crossed it, but I found death on the other side. Oh, God, who made the moose and the antelope, the wapiti and the whitetail, and last and best made the bounding deer, I die among the lowland shadows, but by the light of my death I see my sins. God of the mountains who made the sunrise, also, accept my spirit in your pastures among your pale mountains where the water is blue and still, and where the flesh-eaters never wait by the salt licks, and where man never comes, and it is always dawn. . . ."

"Amen," said the golden coyote, shivering a little as he heard the last phrase.

The mule deer did not speak again. Its head had fallen. The wind ruffled its hair, and its eyes were filled with the sunrise, but the coyote knew that it was dead.

Now he looked back across the creek, where the two wolves were running up and down, jumping and yelping in their frantic disappointment. The coyote mounted a rock so that his voice could be heard more clearly.

"Cousins," he said, pitching the words so that they would pass across the thunder of the stream, "how shall I thank you? And how you disprove the old saying, that charity sets a bare table. I thought that charity seldom left her own cave, and yet here I find her on the edge of Poplar Creek."

"You eater of moldy mice!" screamed lop-ear.

"Therefore, you give me venison for a change," said the golden coyote. "Many a wolf can give good advice, but very few will give a good meal."

"Half-breed! Half-breed!" yelled lop-ear's wife. "Son of a yellow dog!"

The golden coyote was proud of his self-control, but now he showed his teeth. Trust a female tongue to strike the deepest.

"Well," said the coyote, "I am sorry to see that you would take back your gifts. Come over the water, at least, and help me dine. How wisely you brought down the mule deer to me. I thought he was running in the sky, but my clever cousins brought him down to me. How wisely and well you hunted. Five minutes' conversation with you, my masters, is better than a year's study of trails. Though I confess that you sing more than you talk."

For the wolves now were babbling in high-pitched rage.

"But small speech," said the coyote, "is the sign of much wisdom. Yet haven't I heard that a wise wolf keeps on good terms with his stomach as well as his wife. However, a good digestion is better than proverbs. I only add, as I leave you to invite the banqueters, that the greatest wisdom is the knowledge of one's follies."

He turned and trotted up the slope, where the roar of the stream diminished, but the furious yelling of the timber wolves followed him through the hills.

He was very contented. The taste of pleasure was still in his mouth. But yet he turned now and then to look into the north where the golden light reached and withdrew like a cat's paw along the shadowy side of the Kendal Mountains. Lightning, he could have sworn, playing one of its evil tricks, and yet the sky overhead was purest blue, and the sun was up with glorious brightness. However, he told himself that in this full life a coyote must do one thing at a time, and yonder by the bank of Poplar Creek a warm meal was giving tidings of itself to every wind that blew.

So he hurried on to the cave.

When he came to the edge of the little plateau before the cave's entrance, his two sons sprang up from the brush to greet him. They were almost full grown, and a very shapely pair they made, except that their paws and heads looked a trifle too large for their bodies. Of the two, White Foot was very like his mother, but the bigger puppy, ridiculously called Tingle-Toes by the gray beauty, greatly resembled his father. There were golden splashes about him, and his coat, like that of his sire, was extraordinarily long.

Even this favorite, however, was warned away with a growl. It was all very well for them to dance about him with eager questions, but he felt that their mother should have led them out onto the trail long before.

She lay at the mouth of the cave, looking to the north. And now from the brush at the edge of the little hill shoulder, where she had been lying, the golden coyote's three-legged mother came hobbling. She kept her distance when her son was not with the rest of his family, for mothers-in-law are not welcome in a coyote home.

"Well? Well?" snapped the wife.

The golden coyote yawned, for he loved to tease.

"Oh, nothing to speak of," he said. "What's the news here?"

"Nothing at all," she said.

"There's fresh blood on this stone," he observed, sniffing. "A ground squirrel, I believe."

"White Foot caught it," said the wife. "We've had some grasshoppers, too, if you call that news."

"Humph!" said the father of the family. He touched noses with his mother and lay down beside her.

"Where is it?" she whispered.

"Be quiet," he replied. "There's time for everything. She's in a beastly temper, isn't she?"

"As usual," said the peacemaker.

"If only Tingle-Toes would show the slightest sense on a trail," said the wife, "we wouldn't be half starved all the time, But he must jump up and startle the food right out of our mouths. There was a perfectly delicious mountain grouse . . .

but I won't talk about it. It's too irritating to have a numskull for a son."

"What the puppy never learns, the coyote never knows," said the mother-in-law calmly. "And, for that matter, teaching others teaches oneself. You ought to go in for their education a little more seriously, my dear, really."

"Education!" cried the gray beauty, the hair bristling along her back. "As if I haven't set him the best example. When I hear you talk . . . I simply pray for patience."

"Yes," said the mother of the golden coyote. "A moment's patience is a ten years' comfort. Be patient, my dear, and you will have patient children. What a word it is . . . patience. Your poor dear uncle," she added to her son, "used to say . . . 'At the bottom of patience is heaven.' "

"But all that he found," snapped the wife, "was the jaw of a trap. Patience my foot! No, it's a beggar's virtue. Tingle-Toes is simply an idiot, the way he hunts. I wish you'd teach him yourself."

"The child will hear you in another moment," said the mother-in-law. "Teach him? Oh, delighted. I've never wished to interfere, you know."

"Except by talking all day long and finding fault!" snapped the young mother.

"Here, here!" said the golden coyote. "Enough of this nonsense."

"Listen!" snapped his wife. "It's very well for you to make thunder on an empty stomach, but I'm tired of your tyrannous ways. Disgusted, too. Little you care about the children. Neither does your mother, offering her horrid comments all day long. What has she done for the children?"

"I've been afraid of touching them for fear you'd cut my throat," she said. "And then . . . dear, dear, how true it is that experience must be paid for. Still, patience, patience, my poor child, and remember that with time and patience the lamb grows into mutton. Which makes harder killing and longer eating."

"There she goes again," said the wife. "If you don't stop her talking, I'll go mad. Tingle-Toes! Stop eating those pebbles! You'll ruin your teeth! How many times do I have to tell you! I never saw such a creature! I never did. It's enough to drive one frantic."

"There's White Foot doing the same thing," said the golden coyote. "Why don't you reprimand him, now and then?"

"Poor thing. No wonder. Half starved all his life," she complained.

The golden coyote leaped to his feet. "Is there any justice and logic in you females?" he said loudly.

"Hush, hush!" exclaimed his wife. "If that is not exactly like the voice of a dog . . . and the children already have heard whisperings. That detestable magpie was here talking at dawn. You must watch your voice, though. Suppose that. . . ."

"What do I care?" rumbled the golden coyote, nevertheless, lowering his tone. "Dogs and coyotes . . . they all go to one heaven, I dare say."

"Ah, is that so?" she said.

"Yes, that's so. And you needn't be so ugly. Besides, nobody really has dared to tell my mother that my father was actually a dog."

"The contemptible gossips," she said, licking the stump of her fourth leg.

The young wife jerked up her head. "I ask you. I ask you now!" she demanded.

The mother of the golden coyote lifted her head in turn. She was growing old and stiff, now. Her sides were perpetually lean, and her coat was turning white, the worst of summer hunting colors. Very little could she kill for herself, now, except an inexperienced mouse, here and there, or a frog, or such watery

not even out of breath."

"Oh, no," said the golden coyote. "I let lop-ear and his wife do the running for me. Let the others do the hunting. I prefer the eating . . . when a coyote comes to my age. Keep in single file, now, and I'll lead the way. What a delightful fragrance of young rabbit in the air. Have you noticed?"

"How could I help?" said the wife happily.

Then, well to the rear, her voice broken by her laboring, three-legged gait, they heard the mother calling: "Do you think it is safe, my dears? There certainly is trouble in the sky!"

Trouble there was. The thunderheads had sped half across the heavens and now and then the voice of the storm rumbled to them faintly, as though underground. Those arms of lightning, which had lain naked along the slopes of the North Kendal Mountains at dawn, were now in the prime of the day confined to the black clouds, or else thrusting sharp lariat lines of crooked light toward the earth.

The golden coyote, however, kept on.

"Follow behind me and do everything that I do," he panted. "When the sky is angry, it is not always at you and me. Avoid green trees in wet places. Shun the poplars and prefer the pines. I think those are the right rules, Mother?"

"Perfectly right," she panted, and still she had energy to pant: "One lesson by rote is worth ten half learned."

They approached Poplar Creek as the fringe of the storm swept over them. The long, dark fingers of the rain rushed and rattled among the trees, then they were gathered into a murky twilight with the lightning pulsing like an irregular heartbeat. It smote among the trees before them. Darkness covered the lofty blue vault of the heavens with a flat, slatey ceiling. The wind was not strong. Only now and again it touched the tops of the highest trees with a roaring like a distant surf, but the lightning struck more thickly, and the thunder burst in awful floods that drowned the senses. Not on the North Kendals, but on the eastern mountains the golden coyote now saw balls of brilliant fire rolling down to the valleys.

To their right, a hundred-foot fir was struck full on the head by a great shaft. Its riches of watery sap were in that instant converted to superheated steam: the flaws of pitch and resin stopped the flow of the electric currents like governors lashed down, and that big trunk, three feet through at the base, exploded like a chunk of gunpowder. Bits of wood and bark were blown toward the file of coyotes, and the puppies howled dismally, and shrank closer to their elders.

"The God of the coyotes is angry," said the golden coyote, "but we are not the only coyotes in the world. Courage, little ones! Courage all!"

He himself flinched to the side, a moment later, as a blinding current twisted around the trunk of a pine. Then another, a giant, was smitten. Shorn in two, the lower half tossed upward a flare of strong flames like a torch. The nose of the golden coyote burned. Every hair stood erect, so loaded was the air with electricity, but still he kept on, for dinner was waiting, and only one call in the wilderness is stronger than that of meat.

He had his reward, for the heart of the storm passed; the lightning showers flashed far behind them. Not even rain fell upon their wet coats, now, but rushed like wind among the distant trees. Then they came to the view of the kill.

They went at it with little murmurs of joy, the wife and the two puppies first; the mother last because she was so far to the rear. The golden coyote waited for her, assuming a distant and indifferent air, as he walked rather stiffly to and fro. It did not become the provider to express joy in his deeds but rather to take everything for granted, as though this were but an ordinary day's work.

In fact, his back was turned, when he heard the metallic

clang of the closing jaws of the trap and the loud yell of Tingle-Toes. As he turned back, frozen with dread, he saw his favorite son wrenching at something that held him fast, and heard the rattling of the chain. Man had been there before them. Aye, now the scent of man reeked up to him from the soil. Five had been in their litter. The forest fire had taken one; rifle bullets had bitten as deep as the life of two more. Only this pair remained, and now one of these was gone, or else maimed for life.

"Steady!" called the voice of the grandmother. "There is nothing to be gained by wrenching. It increases the pain and fixes the jaws deeper. Lie still, poor little one."

The wife leaped high in the air, shrieking to her remaining son. In a loose semicircle they remained in the distance, looking on.

"Do something!" she whined to the golden coyote. "You've always loved him the best, therefore, do something for him now!"

He did not move. He could not move.

"It's true!" she howled at him. "Oh, I've known all along that what they said is true. Half-breed! Son of a yellow dog!"

That taunt overmastered him. He rushed in blindly, and jerked to a stop as a mouth leaped at him from the ground and bitter teeth of iron were fixed in a hind leg. The ring of the snapping trap sounded in his ears like a death song; the long arm of man had reached to him at last. And, from behind, he heard a loud, clattering outcry that reminded him of the scolding of crows.

"A clumsy fool . . . such a thing for a husband," he heard the wife saying. "White Foot, stay back. Gracious heavens, what can we do for him now, except to be caught in the same teeth. No, no, the lightning was not a warning to us. Oh, he knew, he knew. And now one more of my precious sons gone. I thank heaven that it was not White Foot!"

The golden coyote turned. He was caught at the hock. The pain was exquisite, and the teeth worked slowly, softly deeper, grinding against the bone. He was lost; vaguely he wished that Tingle-Toes would stop crying like a cowardly puppy. Then he heard a deep, gruff voice, almost as deep as the voice of a bear.

"Wolves!" cried his wife. "White Foot! White Foot! Do you hear me? Run for your life! He knew so much, let him care for his own life now. Run . . . follow me. . . . Yellow dog . . . half-breed, you. . . ."

She fled with her tail between her legs; White Foot streaked behind her. This was her love.

And yonder, out of the shadows among the trees, appeared the great head and the lofty shoulders of lop-ear, the timber wolf. Tingle-Toes, with a new yell of fear, climbed over the mule deer, and dragged his chain to the side of his father.

"Good," said lop-ear. "I was waiting to see how fast a quick runner could come to trouble. The lighter the foot, the shorter the way. But man shall not have the trouble of killing you, yellow dog. I, lop-ear, will talk to you a little closer. Swallow, swallow, my friend, and see if you can learn the taste of your own blood."

The golden coyote looked at the puppy. It was whimpering with terror, and helpless. There would be no help from him, but now, stealing softly, trembling with fear of the ground, came the whitened mother. She reached him safely, and crouched at his side.

"I am here, little one," she said. "I for his legs, and you for his throat. The old hold and the strong hold, and the God of the coyotes is seeing it all."

The golden coyote laughed with lolling red tongue, and the lightning flickered into his eyes from far off.

"Come, cousin," he said to the stalking wolf. "Your weight is that of all three of us. And one of us has only half a tooth. But come in, and welcome. Mind the teeth that man has planted in the ground. Come and taste us. There is blood here, lop-ear."

The timber wolf circled them. There was strength in his jaws to break their necks. There was weight in his shoulders to beat them, all three, to the earth at a single stroke. But the fear of man lay on the ground where he stepped, and made him shudder. He circled, and the three turned with him, showing three sets of bared teeth.

"Why should I waste myself?" asked lop-ear. "I shall wait here until man comes and gives you a bullet apiece. I shall wait here and listen when you pray. Pray now to the God of the coyotes, and listen as the God of the wolves laughs at you. Do you hear?"

The thunder pealed on the southern hills, and lop-ear sat down on his haunches.

"I am dying," moaned the puppy. "My blood runs down my leg. The bone is breaking. I am dying, Father. Teach me what to do."

"Listen to me as I pray," said the golden coyote, "and say amen at the end. There is nothing more that we can do, for man has taken us, and his teeth of iron never fail, and his iron jaws never relent."

"Yes, pray," mocked the wolf. "I am here to listen."

"Well, well, well, well!" said a voice from a tree above them. "This is a touching picture. I have seen it before, but what is so dear to us as the familiar scene?"

The golden coyote looked up and saw first the naked, raw neck of a buzzard, then the heavy-winged shoulders, and all of the gruesome bird, which half melted into the shadowy branches of the fir.

"Are you there, undertaker?" said the golden coyote, and shuddered at his own words.

"Here at last," wheezed the buzzard. "I have been watching for days and days. I am as empty as a draw in August. I am as light as hollow bones and feathers can make me, but the God of the buzzards watches over his own."

"What is it?" asked the puppy, whining.

"I, my child," said the buzzard, "am the ultimate. Others begin, but I am the end of all things. All that fly and all that run at last come home to me. Beauty, and speed, and courage, and strength, are all put on the earth and flung into the air for my sake."

"And what are you?" said the puppy.

"I am that which burns over the desert and freezes above the snows of the mountains," said the buzzard. "I am the eternal eye, and the eternal hunger. Or, in another sense," he went on, ruffling his hard, strong feathers like dead leaves, "in another sense I am the remover of unessentials who reduces things to the necessary skeleton of facts. If you would understand me, in one word I am the enemy of pretense, the searcher after truth, the hater of fleshly shams and shows, whether in the blue sky, or on the green earth. I am too much of a philosopher to enjoy repeating myself, but I may state again for a youthful mind that I am the end."

"Tell him," said the timber wolf, "where you begin."

"I begin," said the buzzard, "on those shallow deceivers, those impudent spies and falsifiers, those fickle windows to the eternal brain. . . ."

"You'll have to get down to words of one syllable," declared the wolf.

"Very well. I begin on the eyes," said the buzzard, and stretched his neck, and gaped in a horrible fashion. Then he settled back and clicked his beak.

"All of you . . . all three of you," said the timber wolf. "He and his friends will have you all."

"Heaven bless my empty maw," said the buzzard. "And you, too, my big friend."

The timber wolf jumped aside, with a snarl. "You ugly ghost!" he cried.

"Beauty," said the buzzard, "I don't pretend to, being merely a poor lover and seeker after truth. The outsides of things are of little interest to me, including my own. But the inner light is what I strive to find. . . ."

"God of the coyotes," said the golden coyote.

"The weak coward is going to pray," said the timber wolf.

"Hush," said the buzzard. "Faith is always beautiful. How often has nothing but faith sustained me."

"God of the coyotes," said the father, "if my life has been displeasing to you, take it then, and do with it as you will. But this is my son. He is young. He is innocent. My blood is his blood. His blood is my blood. Let the bullet of man find me, and the maw of the buzzard receive me. As for my spirit, let it wander as you will through eternal snows where not even crickets are living, or let it run again among the good, fat smells of heaven. But permit the little one to live. Weaken the jaws of the trap. Let him go. Amen."

"Amen," moaned the grandmother.

"Do you hear?" asked the golden coyote.

But Tingle-Toes looked him in the face. Then he stood up and shook himself, and his chain rattled.

"I, also," he said, "am a coyote."

It seemed as though Providence had been waiting for this, as for a signal. A rifle clanged from the thicket. The golden coyote heard the bullet strike with a thud, as of a heavy rock falling a distance into mud, and Tingle-Toes dropped lifeless, with a bullet through his brain. At that report, the buzzard rose slowly, with heavily flapping wings, squawking in terror, and the timber wolf fled with a great howl.

Man in person stood lofty in the clearing, with the metal death glimmering in his hand.

At this, the mother flattened herself against the ground and bared her teeth.

"I shall die with you, my son," she said. "I shall not run. Oh, God of the coyotes, that I could give my hollow old life for your beautiful, strong, and young one."

"You cannot give it to me," said the golden coyote. He licked the face of the dead puppy, and then stood above him, confronting man, who is death. "You cannot save me, Mother," he said. "Save yourself, but only tell me first the truth. Am I true of my kind, pure in blood, honest in my line? Am I a coyote, or am I crossed with the blood . . . of a yellow dog?"

He listened. But she only whimpered, and would not reply.

"It is true," said the golden coyote, and his heart stood still.

Man came nearer, strangely balancing upon two legs, awkward, crushing the leaves and the soil with his odd tread. And his voice sounded close, as before the coyote had heard it.

"By the eternal . . . ," he said. "The golden coyote again . . . aye, and the three-legged mother. And his puppy, is it, that he's guarding? My luck in a trap? No, no, lad, I'll never take you until you come freely home to me." He strode closer.

The golden coyote stiffened himself to receive a shock. Spring he could not, though he knew by a voice within him where life lay softly covered in the throat of man, but a sense of old time, and a ghostly message out of another life, overwhelmed him. He could not leap.

The foot of man came forward and stepped on the spring; the golden coyote drew his wounded leg from the teeth.

"Now, git," said man, and waved his hand.

The golden coyote crouched by the body of his son and waited, not even baring his teeth. From the edge of the brush he heard the gasping whine of his mother.

"Come, come quickly before his eye is on you. Quickly, my son, for the God of the coyotes has heard one part of your prayer."

Still he did not move. It was man who drew back.

"Coyote be danged," he said. "There's not so much heart in the whole sneakin' race. Go your own way, my boy, but the time'll come when you lick my hand, like your father before you."

He was gone. The dead lay near. The cold of the ground was in it, and stealing into the body of the golden coyote, also, but he listened to the retreating footfall of man as it crunched on a dead, fallen branch, and squashed with a sucking sound in mud, then went muffled over the soft grass beyond. He listened, and thought of the shining windows of the house, the soul-appeasing warmth within it, and the sound of voices.

VI

He was not hungry, and, therefore, he did not walk in covert but took the open way, partly because it was the shortest and easiest route, and partly because there would be voices in the air speaking about him, which was his continual delight. Nothing pleased his mother so much as this hymn of praise, or of recognition, at least, as she hobbled along with humped back and age-stiffened loins behind her lordly son. It was the very finest moment of the day, when the smoky dawn is freshening with rose and the black trees turn green. The cold dew upon the ground was enriched by many scents, but mostly he lifted his head to listen to the murmurs of the swiftly flowing river of bird life that passed through the air.

A flight of sparrows, dipping up and down, dropped a pattering fall of chirrupings about his head, like musical rain. A low-skimming owl swayed up into the air, hovered, and slanted off again with a long, deep note. A red-shouldered hawk dropped out of the sky and spoke harshly above him. So it was every moment, to say nothing of the blue jays and the magpies, his constant attendants, those wise followers of the most successful hunters, and what he heard from them all, and what the ground squirrel yipped from the distance, and the tree squirrel grumbled above him, and the whisper in the grass that withdrew on either side of him like softly retiring waves was always: "The golden coyote! The golden coyote!"

He lolled his red tongue and blinked. There was no food like the taste of his own majesty.

Said his mother behind him, panting and grunting rather from the habit of weariness than because she was weary now: "Even these fools in this foolish world . . . they begin to know you, my son."

"Tush," he said. "Mere chatter, I should say."

His mother accepted this challenge, as mothers usually do. "Well," she said, "there was a time when the grizzly was called the king of the Musquash Valley . . . now they speak of the golden coyote."

He was flattered almost to blindness, but he said lightly: "Compared with the grizzly, what am I? A mere wisp of bones and a puff of fur. There is lop-ear, too, who is more than twice my size. He could break my back with one bite. And then the skunk-bear. . . ."

"*Faugh!* That carrion eater!" said the mother in disgust. Then she went on—loving this debate because she knew that she would win it. "As for the timber wolves, the whole valley laughs at the way you made them hunt for you . . . as for the grizzly, with his man's foot and pig's nose, what of the day when he ran from the rattler and you killed it? But the whole valley talks, and I know what it says. I have ears as well as a nose, I thank heaven, and I know that they are still hunting and murmuring about your voyage down the river when it was in flood . . . and how you entered the forest fire . . . and how you trapped the dogs . . . and how you climbed the tree . . . and of the great antelope run in the Black Desert . . . and how you crossed the North Kendal Mountains through the bitter snow . . . and of how. . . ."

"Well," said the golden coyote, "I suppose they don't forget to gossip about my divorce, either?"

"The fool!" she answered. "I never yet saw a pretty face that had a brain behind it. She was too busy thinking of her bright eyes and her charming silver-gray complexion to make either a good mother or a good wife. But time," she added bitterly, "will turn silver and russet, and gold, also, to the same dirty shade of white that I now wear. If ever she lives to such a dignity of years."

"Hush," said the golden coyote. "You were speaking of dogs, a moment ago."

The wind, puffing gently from the southeast, carried to them the far-off baying of dogs that seemed the conversing of a whole hunting pack at first, but, when the echoes were sorted away, there remained only two voices on the trail.

"Man is hunting," said the mother, the hair rising along her back.

"No," answered her son critically. "They are running too fast and steadily for man to be with them, hobbling along on only two of his wretched legs."

"The pitiful creature!" snarled the mother.

"The bully and unseen murderer," replied the golden coyote.

"Heaven be praised," she said, "that man no longer exercises his strange fascination over you . . . it was like the snake and the bird, say I, and. . . ."

"You say too much," he replied tartly. "Is that a chipmunk on the wind?"

"Yes. But I'm tired of that meat."

Close by, a solitaire began to sing from the top of a tree.

"Where are those dogs running?" asked the mother.

"Down Beaver Creek . . . may they break their legs among the rocks . . . but now be quiet and listen to this bird."

"I have heard better," she muttered.

As though he had heard this comment, the solitaire commenced one of his lyrical outbursts, the power of his song lifting him again and again into the air, from which he dropped softly back to his treetop with outspread wings. Apart from the jeweled setting of his music, his words had little meaning, and, like the rich, tumultuous music itself, they were jumbled, full of repetitions, but they ran somewhat as follows:

"Greatest of all gods, God of the thrushes, the hermit thrush, the veery, the robin, the blackbird, the solitaire, all-strong and all-wise lover of melodies . . . berries and ripe fruits on the autumn trees are all of Your giving . . . the spring ground is filled with soft worms and with grubs . . . each mouthful is a life matured and ripened by Thee for my sake. Oh, good world, young, young, young . . . never aging. My music masters the falling waters and the singing wind in the cañons. Chorusing frogs and crickets keep the undersong. Love, undying, undying, I sing in your honor, also. And the golden warm midday, and the sweet chill of the morning, and the soft-winged twilight . . . the valley shadows, and the bright, cold mountain heads . . . the pale, clear, dangerous sky, and the comfort of gray mist. Listen to me, oh, God of the thrushes! My song is the most beautiful, oh, world. I, the solitaire, on the bending treetop."

"Silence!" snarled the mother coyote.

Her son whirled, with instinctively bared teeth, and growled at her. But he controlled himself.

"How do you do, my poor, dear earthbound friends?" said the solitaire. "Did you speak?"

"I beg your pardon," said the golden coyote, "for this interruption in the midst of your composition, but my mother had a twinge of rheumatism, I think."

"I never mind interruptions," said the solitaire. "Every new beginning is a better one, and my delight is in continually surpassing myself."

"I never heard such rot," said the mother coyote.

"Hush, Mother," said the golden coyote, ashamed.

"Oh, let us have opinions by all means," said the solitaire. "He who is beyond criticism is beyond learning. What do you object to in my poetry and music, madam?"

"The formlessness," she answered, "the freeness of the verse . . . the head-over-heels tumbling of your thoughts."

The solitaire crooned forth a musical laughter. "Is it possible," he said, "that you are a worshiper of the old, outworn fashions? Tell me your favorite music, although I could almost guess the names beforehand."

"Like any sober-minded person," she said, "I prefer the grave, Doric chorus of the frogs."

"Let me see," said the solitaire. "I have heard it many times, and, yet, it is so long since I have allowed it to fade into the background of my mind that I scarcely remember the words. It runs like this, doesn't it . . . 'God is great, and in God alone is greatness. We proclaim Him, dwellers between air and water, watchers of the stars, how great is God, and near us the dark maiden, death.' Yes, I think those are the words, and I don't deny that they have a certain rhythm."

"Thank you," said the coyote. "As a matter of fact, it is blank verse, as anyone with half an ear can tell."

"I won't argue," said the solitaire. "However, you may as well notice that the frogs never sing new words."

"There is nothing better than the best," answered the mother coyote. "Besides, repetition may rub off gilding, but it only polishes gold."

"You have a patient disposition," said the solitaire. "At this rate, I suppose you will be admiring the songs and stories of the grasshoppers?"

"I like them very well, indeed," she said. "Their stories always have a tragic ending, which is the only proper kind."

"Well," replied the songster, "they always end with the first frost. For my part, I believe in cheerfulness, in love. . . ."

"Then why don't you sing a dignified love song, like the doves?"

"Ah, you mean that mournful chant of theirs . . . 'Oh, love, oh, love, sweet love and gentle death.' Repeated over and over."

"I have spoken of repetitions once before," said the mother coyote sharply, "and I trust that one good answer is enough for you. Unless you are one of these chatterers. The dove song is exquisite, satisfying, and easily remembered . . . three good points in a row."

"It is too grave . . . and there is so much death in it."

"Death is the one general fact in life," said the she-wolf. "The most beautiful day brings one a step closer to the eternal darkness. These themes should be accepted by true poets. As for mere lyrical babbling like yours, without depth, truth, or profound beauty, it really chills me to the stomach."

"Nonsense, Mother," murmured her son.

"Will you tell me why?" asked the courteous solitaire.

"Because it presents youth as the only good. Since I reached middle age, I've never listened to a solitaire without losing my appetite for at least three days. To put this in better language, when I listen to you, I almost forget that life is development and progress, and feel that the only good age is the age of a fool, and not that which wisely knows folly. But life is, in truth, a great and still river that runs down from the hills and at last joins a shadowy but eternal sea. You speak with the lightness of youth, but, if you ever attain to my age, you will understand what I mean when I speak of standing upon an infinite shore."

"I don't doubt you," said the solitaire. "But I can't argue. I can only be. My dear friends, I admire and am interested by the introvert, but I myself have an extraverted mind that pours itself out on many subjects. The whole world . . . I would that I could see it at a glance, so that I could love it all in one instant. But I am not what I will, but what I must be. My own conviction is that at my birth the God of the thrushes gave me for a soul a little of His own breath, and, therefore, all my life I must be returning the loan. I beg your pardon, but I simply cannot talk another instant. I must sing!"

With that word, he fairly exploded upward into the air, and uttered a note of such piercing joy that the golden coyote sat down on quivering haunches. So it was that, looking upward, he saw the dropping line of darkness, and barked a quick warning. But the solitaire was drowned and blinded by his own sweet music. There was a hiss of wings, and a peregrine falcon, with sharp talons, struck the poor minstrel from ecstasy to death. She descended almost to the ground with the force of her stroke, but, rebounding, she lighted upon the very treetop that had been the pulpit of the thrush, plumed her quarry, and made a mouthful of the limp, delicate, little body.

"You observe what comes to these blind rejoicers," said the mother coyote. "To me, I can't help saying, such an ending is fitting. It restores my appetite." She stepped forward and licked from the dewy grass a drop or two of red. Then she raised her head and said with a grin: "What is your song, stranger? For my part, I never have seen your like before, and, therefore, I haven't the slightest idea what your voice is like."

"It is well known in the upper air, however," replied the peregrine, in a tone that reminded the golden coyote of the mourning of a distant storm. "As for singing, I disdain it. I may say that I have eaten several hundred songs in my time, but, though they digested easily, they have left me with no more than an anatomical interest in music, as you might say."

"Exactly," she said. "I understand and delight in your point of view. What are your interests, madam?"

"I am a warrior, a wanderer, and an Amazon of the upper air," said the peregrine. "My home is on mountains, tall trees, or the edge of cliffs where the sea thunders . . . but my real dwelling is among the pinnacles of the highest clouds, where the goddess of the falcons, the maker and ruler of all things, spreads her wings close above me. My love is battle. My duty is to bring down from the blue, death to the weak as well as to the inept."

A gust of wind made the treetop nod, and the hawk spread her long, narrow wings to maintain a balance.

"Death, do you see," said the mother, "is the proper business of life, as I was saying a moment ago to that foolish vaudevillian, that cheap song-and-dance artist. This, now, is a person of importance. I never saw a finer pair of wings."

"And you never will," said the peregrine. "The more closely you examine me, the more perfectly you will find me made for speed. If you look closely at my tail and my wing feathers and talons, you will see that all is ideal about me, and, when I leave you, I advise you to watch me ringing and waiting on above the next lake, where I intend to rob a fish hawk, the moment that the fool rises with food."

"A good many of those words I don't understand," said the golden coyote.

"I never trouble to explain myself," she said. "It is doubtless the first time you have spoken with a haggard, and probably will be the last. As for my vocabulary, it includes many words that among lesser birds have become obsolete and that the poor earth crawlers who never have known the joy of walking the air would not understand without a long lecture. There soars the fish hawk and I am off."

She dipped off the top of the tree as she spoke, disappearing above the woods, while immediately afterward the coyotes saw an osprey rising in labored circles before it headed away to its nest, with the glitter of a fish hanging from its talons. At this, the coyotes could not help licking their lips, for they were fond of that diet and rarely enjoyed it. They had lain for hours on the bank of a lake and through the bushes studied the maneuvers of the osprey with admiration and consuming envy. Sitting on a branch of a tall tree, perhaps where the bluff gave an added elevation, the fish hawk was ready to drop like a stone into the water. There was a loud sound, a silver dashing of spray, and up mounted the osprey with a good fish gripped by the back and pointed straight ahead to lessen wind resistance. Before the noise of its plunge had done echoing, it was out of sight, swiftly winging across the dark heads of the forest. That brightly remembered picture returned on the minds of the watchers as they saw the osprey flying now. Presently the falcon rose into view, not driving directly after the other hawk, but swimming in circles within the great horizon like a fish around a blue pool.

She mounted rapidly, narrowed her circle, towered to the insignificance of a drifting leaf. The osprey had taken alarm, at last, and redoubled its pace, but the falcon glanced down from the middle sky. The loaded fish hawk dodged, and that other graceful pirate of the air, shooting a hundred yards below her mark, glanced up again with widespread wings to a great height above the quarry.

"The first was a warning. This time she means business," said the old mother. "See . . . there she tips. I saw the sun glance on her wings. *Hai,* my son! Suppose we could drop at rabbits and deer in this manner, and run from mountaintop to mountaintop like a trout swimming through the mirror of his lake."

In her second stoop, the hawk fairly dissolved in air to a thin pencil stroke. The osprey shifted, but could not foot fast enough, burdened as she was. The falcon struck so hard that she glanced off at an angle, leaving a puff of feathers to blow on the wind. This was quite enough for the fisher, for she released the prize. It fell like a glistening drop of water, and the falcon, tipping over, scooped it up at the very edge of the treetops. After all this, a small sound came down the breeze, and the coyotes knew that it was the screech of the stricken osprey, now staggering drunkenly down for shelter.

But here both watchers lost all interest in this aerial tragedy, for on the same wind that carried the cry of the fish hawk they heard the dogs giving tongue close by, like two deep-throated bells. The white mother arched her back like a cat.

"They have turned from Beaver Creek into the valley of the Musquash," said her son, "and it's plain to hear them calling . . . 'Coyote! Coyote!' Run for the cave. Even if they like your trail better than mine, I haven't a doubt that they will stop to play, if I remain here and ask them."

Her hair bristled. "Oh, my son, he who puts his head in the wolf's mouth . . . ," she began.

"They are not wolves," he answered. "They're fat-bellied, slow-footed, ignorant mouse killers. They run a pound to catch an ounce, and, if they put so much as a tooth on me, let the whole valley laugh at me, from the Black Desert to the Kendal Woods. Run, now, and take the longer way home, for your three legs make slow work of climbing over steep rocks."

She panted with eagerness to be off, but, somehow, her fear for him made her linger. "To despise danger is to invite death," she told him.

"According to your own story, that is the proper end of life," he reminded her. "But don't fear for me. I shall play such tag with them that the story of it shall be written in red on their hides. Trust me . . . and now be off."

"I go," said the mother. "Only, be no braver than your size. Wise, and brave, and beautiful." She murmured this over her shoulder, and then labored away, whining with effort.

Her son at once shifted to a higher piece of ground from which he commanded a wide view of the woods. In one place they thinned, and he looked through the dusky colonnade to the flash of the Musquash beyond.

The noise of the dogs now rang at his ear; it slid along the ground and rose up with a deep vibration immediately beneath him, but he could follow their progress by a sure guide. For above the trees flew a blue jay with harsh laughter, now and again broken by the distress cry that birds utter when they wish for help against the owl or the intrusive hawk. Those cries of the jay had gathered a number of birds that fluttered and hovered over the treetops like a gust of scattered leaves, and, although when they came nearer, the strident and mocking laughter of the jay told them that they had come in vain and that they might as well be about their business. Yet in spite of their better senses, they had to linger to see this supreme actor, this cruel comedian and clown of the air, who never seems to have anything to do except perform for the entertainment of others—and then rob the homes of his audience, if he can. This jay was an old acquaintance of the coyote who he had followed on hundreds of hunting expeditions for the sake of a few shreds of fresh meat, here and there. His very flight was now full of antics, for sometimes he darted in a straight line, a flash of bright blue, and sometimes he tumbled down like a young bird that has lost balance, though after each pretended fall, which made the little birds in the distance lift in air to watch, his laughter was sure to break out more harshly than ever. In the meantime, he kept up an ironic conversation at the expense of the dogs, saying: "Well jumped, Rusty . . . well run, Gray Tom! Come closer, little ones, and see them working. Their eyes are as red as their tongues.

They are running so fast that the wind has carried away their brains, for they are hunting a dinner of coyote meat today!"

Here the two dogs broke out into the open. They were a mongrel pair, half greyhound and half mastiff, armed with the jaw power of wolves but usually too slow to be dangerous unless the rifle of man was behind them. Gray Tom was richly dappled, but Rusty was a solid black who got his name through the sun-fading of the hair along his back. They ran nose down on the trail that the coyotes had followed, but, coming to a big fallen tree trunk, the golden coyote noted that they did not leap the obstruction as he had done, but turned and ran around it on the course of the time-stiffened mother, so that it was plain that she was their selected prize. Of what value that age-starved body could be to them he could not imagine; the vagaries of dogs were beneath his contempt.

Nose down still, they were rushing by, always calling out the same words in unison, or, one getting a bit behind in that eternal chorus, making a round of it.

"It is on the ground . . . it is in my brain . . . run, run! It is fresher and nearer, run!"

"Brothers, how beautifully you sing," said the golden coyote, stepping out from the brush that had concealed him.

They checked themselves so stiffly that they tore the soft turf. Lumberingly they came about, their red eyes blazing, their jaws a-drip, but he minded them so little that he could afford to listen to the delighted screech of the blue jay above him and to mark the little choristers in the distance blown upward in a whirl of excitement.

"Shoulder to shoulder," he heard Rusty pant to his brother. "And beware of tricky dodging."

He smiled at them out of half-closed eyes. He stood at ease until they were half the length of his own body away, opening their jaws for the stroke, then he leaped to the side, and, as

Rusty went by, he sliced the flank of that monster as if with a razor.

They whirled with howls of rage. They charged in blind fury. But as a beating hand drives the leaf before it, so the very wind of their assaults appeared to waft the coyote here and there before them, while more than once he had a chance to give a good tug with his teeth, or a side rip, after true coyote style.

At last, they drew back, bleeding, insane with fury, and the golden coyote listened to the twittering applause of the songsters, and looked up to where the blue jay tottered with drunken excess of joy in mid-air.

"Save the bones for me to pick!" shouted the jay. "Fight, Rusty! Fight, Gray Tom! In at him with a will! You almost had him then! Down with the little yellow streak of insult." And then he squawked and choked and almost burst with hideous laughter.

The coyote stretched himself on the grass and sniffed with elaborate casualness at a twig that had been overturned in the trampling.

"This is a very good game for those who know it," he said to the panting dogs. "What a pity that you come out so seldom to play with me." He pricked his ears. More birds were coming; he heard their voices in a sweetly pattering rain of applause and curiosity.

"Leave him," said Gray Tom. "As well chase a cloud of mosquitoes. And the half-bred cur is laughing at us."

The golden coyote stood up, his back humped with wrath. "Half-breed?" he said, with curling lips.

The blue jay danced above them, his wings translucent with sunlight. "Slander! Slander!" he cried.

At this, Rusty looked up. "They know. The whole forest knows," he said. "And why shouldn't we, who saw your father every day of his life except when he went out maundering through the woods and grew sentimental about the wild things that were the death of him, in the finish."

"No doubt you knew him," said the coyote, "and no doubt he wrote his name in your skin as I have done today."

"Tell him," said Rusty. "I'm out of breath."

"I have driven him," answered Gray Tom, "both from hidden bones, and from his own portion of raw meat."

"You lie!" cried the coyote.

"He lies, lies!" laughed the blue jay overhead. "Come closer and everyone listen!"

In fact, the little chirruping cloud of songsters floated nearer with a purring of many wings.

"Your father," said Gray Tom, panting and grinning at the same time, "was a poor, skinny, unconsidered, sentimental sheep dog, forever whining about the wilderness and wanting to hear stories about wolves. A contemptible creature, always hanging about the house and licking the hand of man, and being kicked out of the way. A frightful bore in the kennel, so that we were glad when he went away and tried his hand at being a coyote."

"All lies," said the golden coyote. But the very marrow of his bones ached with cold apprehension.

"Be off, now," said Gray Tom to his companion. "There's the old one still before us."

They galloped away side-by-side, heads down, and, as the rocks and brush closed behind them, they threw up a loud and musical confusion of baying once more.

The coyote stood, bewildered and sick at heart. Many a time, in rage or in derision, the birds and the beasts had called him "yellow dog." Even his wife, when she left him, had cast that final insult in his teeth, and it was a question that his mother never would answer directly.

A sheep dog, then, one of those caretakers of the white-wooled fools whose throats were as easily slit as naked fat. A poor slave, half starved, working for no reward but an opportunity to kiss the hand of the master. And what was he, the golden coyote, in that case, no more than a runaway servant that one day might be reclaimed by man? The hair prickled and bristled along his back, but he recalled himself to his duty.

"Brother," he said to the blue jay, "rise over the shoulder of that hill and tell me where the pair are hunting, and where my mother runs."

"Certainly," said the blue jay with unnecessary loudness. "And don't be a whit down-hearted. There's many a famous bar sinister in history, and what are the two of them but mongrels?" He chuckled as he rose, and, flirting away over the hillside, he dipped back again at once. "Three legs never ran better," said the blue jay, "but they're closing on her, and they certainly will have her before she gains the cave."

At this, the golden coyote forgot his troubles. Or rather, he translated them into the headlong speed with which he scaled the slope. Crossing it, he heard the dog voices before him with such a howling note as when they closed on a staggering deer. He ran faster than ever, the loose hide rippling on his back with every stretch of his supple body.

The blue jay dipped down on an easy wing, crying: "Hurry, hurry! They are just beyond the aspen grove! Hurry all you little ones, too, for this will be something to see!"

And, at his call, the songsters whirred up on wings that grew invisible with rapid pulsation; over the farther edge of the wood they showered away out of sight like leaves on a falling wind. The slender trunks and the bright foliage of the aspens were faintly flushed, like a winter cloud by the sunrise color. Through it he rushed, and on the farther side he saw the three.

They almost had her at that moment, but yet on her three legs she could dodge, and so doubled back toward him with gaping mouth and her eyes green. He went by her like a noise in the wind, hearing her gasp: "A fleet foot is better than strong teeth. Strike and away. The old game, child."

He barely heard her, for he was seeing with all his mind the picture of a sheep dog cowering away from his food before the rush of these great brutes. And a fighting instinct to close and grapple mastered him, sweeping away in an instant all those graceful and dangerous lessons in fencing that his wise mother had taught him long ago.

It was absurdly simple. The mouth of Rusty gaped wide enough to swallow his slender body, but he dipped under that bulky head and locked his jaws on the throat.

He was flung here and there, crashing through a bush, thumped heavily against a log, but he closed his eyes and worked deeper toward the life. Then agony fastened on his right flank.

It was Gray Tom who had him with a grip that encompassed half his body and poured all his vitals full of fire. Rusty flung backward in a last struggle. The golden coyote was strung on a rack between the two, yet he kept the good deep grip until the black dog suddenly crumpled. The rigid power melted from his limbs, he fell loosely to the ground, and the coyote knew he never would rise again.

So he loosed his hold and turned as well as he could. The white old mother had worked her broken teeth into a leg of Gray Tom so that his back was humping with pain, and, when the golden coyote slashed him across the face, Tom had enough. He leaped back, with his jaws red stained. He tucked his tail between his legs and fled with a howl.

The coyote did not follow. His hind legs buckled beneath him, and he lay down on the grass while his mother came to sniff the wound.

"All this for me!" she whimpered. "I who have less remaining in me than a grasshopper in November. Oh, my beautiful and brave, my golden son, tell quickly where the pain runs."

"It is in all my body, but mostly in my brain," he said.

She licked his face, whining, but he turned his head and regarded steadily the hopeless ebbing of the blood from his side.

"You are going to live," she told him. "The good Father of the coyotes, would he pass over my wretched last drop of existence in order to take you in the midst of your strength and your loveliness, my son?"

"Is the God of the coyotes my God?" he asked her bitterly. "Or is it the God of dogs to whom I should pray? Or am I a wretched mongrel shut out from both worlds?"

She did not answer, and he would not look at her. He closed his eyes and dropped his head upon his paws. Then out of the darkness she spoke to him, saying: "When he came into the valley and called to me the first time, I thought I had been waiting all my life to hear his voice. When I looked down into the shadows, it seemed to me that a golden thing had run up the Musquash out of the sunset sky, and how could I help but go down to him, my son?"

He quoted softly: "Oh, love, oh, love . . . oh, sweet and gentle death."

He closed his eyes again, and it seemed to him that the world unrolled before him, and all the song of the solitaire rang in music at his ears in praise of morning and sunset, and of warm noon, and shadowy twilight. He saw the white-headed mountains, and the softness of the green valleys. He, at one glance, even as in the prayer of the thrush, saw the world and loved it with the love of one for a home that he is about to leave forever.

"Man is the god of dogs, and, therefore, he is my god," he said. "If there is strength enough left in me, I am going down the valley to his cave, and there he may put the magic of his hands upon me and make me whole again."

He rose. It seemed that half his life poured out from his side as he did so, but, after bracing himself for a moment on his numb and failing legs, he began to go down the hill. The blood of Gray Tom led him better than a light, and the white mother went beside him. When they came to the stream, he drank deeply, and saw her face beside his in the water.

"Hush," he said, though she was as still as the softly flowing current. "I forgive you everything. Let us go on."

They went on, side-by-side. He knew that she was striving to be quiet, but every breath from her was a moan, saying: "Faster, faster. Patience and courage, for a great heart is more than blood can drain."

He did not answer. He had no breath to spare.

The red tidings were everywhere, it seemed. On either side of him a whisper ebbed away along the ground. A horned owl swayed above him on wings like a drawn breath, and far away they heard the cry of the timber wolf. Some life was still in him, but he knew that he was the quarry for whom that song was sung.

When he was close to the house, his hind legs sagged beneath him, but, while they shuddered and he threw up his head with effort, he saw far above him the circling buzzard, and, at the sight of that living death, he was able to go on. His mother shrank away from him as he neared the door, but the blue jay perched on the roof ridge, and a magpie dressed in black silk with white facings lighted on the eaves above the door.

Bird song was rippling all through the valley, but the sun was not yet up, though the windows glowed. The smell of wood smoke and hot iron oozed through the cracks of the doors, and, inside, he could hear the muttering and roaring fire, which also was enslaved by the enchanter.

Breathing of these scents, something out of the ancient past came into the mind of the coyote. It was outside of knowledge, but it was like a memory of voices and a touch upon his head.

He whined, and scratched at the door, which opened at once upon wreaths of smoke, some of which clung about the woman who stood there throwing up her hands and crying out. Then came man himself with a heavy, running step that shook the house, and, at the sight of him, the coyote quailed lower on the doorstep. He would have fled, but the last scruple of his strength was gone. Man leaned above him and spoke.

At the sound of this voice, the heart of the golden coyote melted; his tail wagged softly from side to side.

"I said he would come," said man. Then he stooped lower and passed beneath the body of the coyote his hands, and lifted that inert weight. Exquisite agony filled the wounded flesh, beyond belief, but the coyote gave no sign. On the kitchen table they threw a blanket. On the blanket they laid him, but his head pointed toward the open door, and through it he could see chickens strutting in the yard, ducks waddling down to the pond, and beyond, at the corner of the corral fence, sat his old mother, with all her hair bristling.

Something very hot was laid over his wound, so that the chill aching began to end, and in its place a sleepy comfort stole through his veins. Then the hands of man, with the deadly odor of iron strong upon them, wrapped a cloth about his body. After that, his head was raised, his weak jaws parted, and something pungent flowed down his throat. It made his eyes go blind, for a moment. It burned his stomach. The revolting taste of it made him shudder, but afterward a greater comfort followed.

The child came in. There was no fear in her. There never had been, but she took in her arms his fighting head so filled with wisdom, with cunning, and with pain, and she made over him a noise like the crooning of doves and the moaning of a wounded thing. He could hear and feel the throbbing of her heart. She was softer than a puppy of three weeks, and the touch of her hand, stroking his face, was gentler than a mother's tongue.

He looked up and lifted his head, which wavered with weakness, but for some reason he looked not into her weeping eyes, but straight into the stern and scowling face of man. Long and long he stared, until it seemed to him that all the days of his life were stripped away from him, one by one. He felt naked, weak, and blind.

"I have seen the face of my god," said the golden coyote, and he knew that he was about to die.

Outside, he could hear the voices of the wild pigeons on the roof. They were saying: "What is inside? Why do you dare to sit over the entrance to the cave of man?"

"It is the golden coyote," said the magpie crisply.

"Ah, have they managed to kill him at last?" asked the pigeons in their voices that never could be harsh.

"It is far from me to be a gossip, and particularly about a good soul who has furnished me many a meal simply by following his wise footsteps, but I may say that the golden coyote is not dead. I should state it more simply by saying that he has come home, at last."

The man spoke.

The girl drew back.

The great and all-wise hands of man himself took the weight of the coyote's head, and the golden coyote licked them, for he had passed beyond fear.

The sun rose, but to his dim eyes it seemed that it was only the dawning of beautiful knowledge that blinded him and filled him with content more infinite than the murmurings of the broad river where it left the valley and passed into the unbounded desert. For he had raised his voice against man, and bared his teeth against him, and hated him, but man was god, and god, in the end, had forgiven him. He that seemed so terrible and grim was kinder than a good spring day and gentler than a mother's love. This knowledge grew into dazzling brightness, then utter darkness received him.

"Listen," said the voice of man. "That is his mother wailing. She knows. He came to me at last, but he came too late. We never could have him living, but we have him dead. We've been sinful folk, I fear, and the great God forgive us."

ABOUT THE AUTHOR

Max Brand is the best-known pen name of Frederick Faust, creator of Dr. Kildare, Destry, and many other fictional characters popular with readers and viewers worldwide. Faust wrote for a variety of audiences in many genres. His enormous output, totaling approximately 30,000,000 words or the equivalent of 530 ordinary books, covered nearly every field: crime, fantasy, historical romance, espionage, Westerns, science fiction, adventure, animal stories, love, war, and fashionable society, big business and big medicine. Eighty motion pictures have been based on his work along with many radio and television programs. For good measure he also published four volumes of poetry. Perhaps no other author has reached more people in more different ways. Born in Seattle in 1892, orphaned early, Faust grew up in the rural San Joaquin Valley of California. At Berkeley he became a student rebel and one-man literary movement, contributing prodigiously to all campus publications. Denied a degree because of unconventional conduct, he embarked on a series of adventures culminating in New York City where, after a period of near starvation, he received simultaneous recognition as a serious poet and successful author of fiction. Later, he traveled widely, making his home in New York, then in Florence, and finally in Los Angeles. Once the United States entered the Second World War, Faust abandoned his lucrative writing career and his work as a screenwriter to serve as a war correspondent with the infantry in Italy, despite his fifty-one years and a bad heart. He was killed during a night attack on a hilltop village held by the German army. New books based on magazine serials or unpublished manuscripts or restored versions continue to appear so that, alive or dead, he has averaged a new book every four months for seventy-five years. Beyond this, some work by him is newly reprinted every week of every year in one or another format somewhere in the world. A great deal more about this author and his work can be found in *The Max Brand Companion* (Greenwood Press, 1997) edited by Jon Tuska and Vicki Piekarski. His Website is www.MaxBrandOnline.com. His next Five Star Western will be *Sky Blue*.